A FairyTale for EVERYONE

Selected and edited by Boldizsár M. Nagy
Translated by Anna Bentley
Illustrated by Lilla Bölecz

Farshore

First published in Great Britain 2022 by Farshore
An imprint of HarperCollins*Publishers*
1 London Bridge Street, London SE1 9GF
www.farshore.co.uk

HarperCollins*Publishers*
1st Floor, Watermarque Building, Ringsend Road
Dublin 4, Ireland

Text copyright © Zoltán Csehy, Petra Finy, Eszter Gangl, Dóra Gimesi, Sára Harka,
Noémi Rebeka Horváth, Kriszta Kasza, Edina Kertész, Judit Ágnes Kiss,
Brigitta Kovács, István Lakatos, Krisztina Rita Molnár, Edit Pengő, Orsolya Ruff,
Edit Szűcs, Andrea Tompa, Judit B. Tóth, 2020
Illustrations copyright © Lilla Bölecz, 2020
Originally selected and edited by Boldizsár M. Nagy
Originally published in Hungary by Labrisz Lesbian Association, 2020.
Translation by Anna Bentley

ISBN 978 0 00 850820 3
Printed in Latvia.
001
A CIP catalogue record for this title is available from the British Library.

Stay safe online. Any website addresses listed in this book are correct at the time
of going print. However, Farshore is not responsible for content hosted by third
parties. Please be aware that online content can be subject to change and websites
can contain content that is unsuitable for children. We advise that all children are
supervised when using the internet.

MIX
Paper from
responsible sources
FSC™ C007454

This book is produced from independently certified FSC™ paper
to ensure responsible forest management.

For more information visit: www.harpercollins.co.uk/green

Note from the Editor

We all need fairy tales, stories of heroes, fairies and dragons in distant lands, wildly fantastical, yet very much like us. Every society we know about, from ancient times until the present day, has felt a need for them. These stories have winged their way across borders and cultures as freely as migratory birds, changing and taking shape as they did so. We reuse and reinterpret them, sometimes ironically, sometimes seriously, sometimes playfully, sometimes as a form of resistance. This is how stories are kept alive; by constantly changing.

As a result, hundreds and thousands of different versions of a single story existed at once, each carrying with it a unique context and world view. Those tales we know today have accumulated layer upon layer of symbolism from many cultures. The Grimm tales, for example, were edited over four decades, until they essentially served an educational purpose. The same can be said of popular Hungarian folktale collections. Many of these seemingly classic tales have lost their origins and are instead stylised versions of very old stories, retouched with Christian elements. As Tolkien puts it, 'Speaking of the history of stories and especially of fairy stories, we may say that the Pot of Soup, the Cauldron of Story, has always been boiling, and to it have continually been added new bits, dainty and undainty.'

This collection was made because we believe that in order to keep a story alive, it is important for as many people as possible to make use of it. We asked the authors to retell a classic story that was important to them from a personal perspective, reflecting their own experience. They chose their heroes boldly, introducing characters that readers from minority communities or marginalised groups would be able to relate to. We had in mind folk stories that had historically gone against the mainstream, those too radical to make it into popular collections. In every one of the selected stories there is a special kind of force. They are at once personal and collective, ranging in form and content; that soup of Tolkien's is bubbling away in each of them.

The final collection is a truly varied one. The Labrisz Lesbian Association set up a competition to find emerging writers, and out of nearly one hundred entries, nine well-known writers and eight new voices were included. When selecting an illustrator for the book, we were looking for an artist who not only understood and loved the classic fairy tales, but whose inner world was full of magic and fairy dust; this is how we came to choose Lilla Bölecz.

It is our hope that all readers, big and small, will find a story that speaks to them in this anthology. Perhaps, like crumbs dropped in the forest, these stories will set them on the path they need to follow – whatever that is.

Boldizsár M. Nagy

Editor, *Meseország Mindenkié* (*A Fairytale For Everyone*)

Contents

Glossary of Hungarian Words

Kapanyányimonyók (koppo-nyah-nyi-mon-yoke) A wicked dwarf with a long beard from the Hungarian legend *Fehérlófia* (*The Song of the White Mare*).

kifli (ki-fli) A crescent-shaped bread roll.

kolbász (kohl-bahs) A dark red, spicy smoked sausage, like salami, made with paprika.

locsolkodás (lo-chol-ko-dahsh) The tradition of sprinkling or throwing eau de cologne or water on women and girls at Easter.

málé (mah-lay) Ground sweetcorn cooked into a porridge (like polenta).

néni (nay-ni), **bácsi** (bah-chi) At nursery and primary school, Hungarian children call their teachers by their given names, followed by *néni* if the teacher is a woman, and *bácsi* if the teacher is a man. This also applies to other adults outside the family like neighbours and family friends.

pogácsa (po-gah-cha) A small savoury baked item, ressembling a scone flavoured with cheese or pork scratchings.

a range In this book, a range refers to a traditional Hungarian wood-fired stove that you can cook on, bake in and, on cold winter's nights, even sleep on.

túrórudi (too-ro-roo-di) A popular chocolate bar filled with cream cheese.

Eszter Gangl

Autumn Brown

Once upon a time there lived a king and a queen who had no children. One day in autumn, the queen was sitting up in her tower, sewing. When she grew tired of this, she opened the window and looked out despondently. Down below, the trunks of the trees were dark in the gloom of evening, but underneath them, the fallen leaves were golden brown as they caught the last rays of sunshine.

"Oh, how happy I would be if I had a child," the queen sighed. "A baby as golden brown as the autumn leaves, with hair as dark as the tree trunks. Boy or girl, I wouldn't mind. I'd love them, whatever they were."

Before a year had passed, a beautiful baby girl was born to the queen. The child's skin was golden brown, just like fallen leaves in the autumn sun, and her hair was as dark and shiny as the bark of the trees. The queen named her Autumn Brown.

Time went by and Autumn Brown grew bigger. She explored the palace and the nearby woods. She played tag with the children of the court. The queen was pleased to see her only daughter so happy.

Her joy was to be short-lived, however, for no sooner had Autumn Brown turned seven, than the queen fell ill. She died soon afterwards.

The king was left to bring up Autumn Brown alone and his ways were not the queen's. He frowned on his daughter dressing in boy's clothes, on her running around in the countryside at all hours and coming home covered in mud and dust.

A princess should stay in the palace, taking dancing lessons and learning etiquette, he thought to himself crossly.

The king had a magic shaving mirror, which gave him advice on any problem he asked it about. One evening, when Autumn Brown had once again come home plastered in mud from head to toe, the king turned to the mirror for help:

"Mirror, mirror, bright and clear!
She'll be the death of me, I fear!"

The king lamented that Autumn Brown refused to wear pretty dresses, that she preferred to dress like a boy and sneak out to run wild in the gardens.

The mirror replied:

"Lock her up on the highest floor,
And place your guards upon the door."

The king did so, and from that day forward, Autumn Brown's life became miserable. She was not allowed to go anywhere and was forced to wear dresses and take dancing lessons. As time went by, at the mirror's urging, the king imposed further cruelties on her. Sometimes she had to dance for hours without stopping. At other times, when the king decided she was too dirty, he would order the servants to scrub her for hours, while she wept hot tears.

Finally, the king grew weary of trying to turn Autumn Brown into a proper princess, and he again sought advice from the mirror.

This time, the mirror said he should tell a huntsman to take her into the woods and kill her. As proof that he had done it, the huntsman should bring back the girl's heart to show the king.

The king wasted no time. That very morning, he sent Autumn Brown off with the huntsman. But when they reached the woods, she started to cry so bitterly that the huntsman felt sorry for her.

Some wild animal will eat her up, in any case, poor little mite, thought the huntsman. He let her go and took a deer's heart back to the king instead.

Autumn Brown was left alone in the woods with nowhere to go and no one to turn to. *Who would want to take me in?* she wondered sadly.

As it began to get dark, Autumn Brown started to feel afraid. She walked quickly, hoping the wild animals of the woods would not hurt her.

She had been wandering in the woods for many hours and was cold and hungry when she saw a light shining in the distance. She hurried towards it.

In the middle of a small clearing stood a little house; the light she had seen was coming from its windows. Autumn Brown knocked on the door, and when nobody answered, she cautiously pushed it open. There was no one in the house, but in the middle of the room was a table neatly laid for seven. Round about it, against the walls, were seven neatly made beds.

I wonder who lives in this house? I didn't meet a soul on my way here, thought Autumn Brown.

She was hungry and it was now completely dark outside, so she decided that she would stay at the house. She ate a little from each bowl, then lay down on one of the beds. She slept in it for a short while before moving to the next, and so on. The seventh bed was so comfortable that she fell fast asleep.

It was late in the evening when the people who lived in the house returned: seven girls, who had been at the market in town all day, selling the cloth they had woven.

They had just sat down to dinner when one of them asked anxiously, "Who's been eating from my bowl?"

"And who's been using my spoon?" asked another.

"And who's been sleeping in my bed?" asked a third.

They each inspected their bowls, spoons and beds. At last, they found Autumn Brown sleeping, soundly in the seventh bed.

"What a sweet child!" cried one of the girls, but the others

quickly told her to hush. They tiptoed back to the table, ate as quietly as they could, then crept to bed. The seventh weaver girl spent the night moving from bed to bed, sleeping just a little next to each of her companions.

In the morning, Autumn Brown was very alarmed to see the seven weaver girls, but when they gathered around her, smiling, she felt reassured that they meant her no harm.

"Who are you?" they asked.

"I'm Autumn Brown," she replied and told them her story.

"Stay here with us," they said. "We have room for you. We're busy weaving all day. While we're working, you could mend the roof for us, cut wood or go hunting, so there's something to put in the pot in the evening."

Autumn Brown was happy to stay. She had nowhere else to go, and here she would be free to do the things she loved.

Back at the palace, the king was feeling calmer, since the hunter had presented him with the deer's heart. He went on with his life, believing that Autumn Brown was no more. One day, however, he took out the mirror and spoke to it again:

"Mirror, mirror, bright and clear!
What's new in my kingdom? Be sincere!"

The mirror started to tell the king everything that was happening in his kingdom. It talked on and on. Then it said something that almost made the king fall off his throne.

"The princess is living in the woods.
With the weaver girls her life is good.
She carves and whittles all day long.
She's always whistling a happy song."

The king became terribly angry. How could Autumn Brown still be alive? And, what was worse, spending her time in such an appalling fashion, doing men's work?

Determined to destroy her once and for all, the king devised a wicked plan. He disguised himself as a hunter and set off for the woods.

That day was market day and the weaver girls had

already packed up their wares and set off for the town. Autumn Brown had stayed behind because she wanted to go hunting.

She was just coming out of the door when the king arrived.

"Where are you off to, my pretty maid?"

"I'm going hunting," replied Autumn Brown cheerfully. She hadn't recognised the king.

"I was just heading into the woods myself. May I go with you?" asked the king.

Autumn Brown was pleased to have company and set off into the woods with the king. They walked and walked until they came to a deep ravine.

"I wonder how we can get across?" said Autumn Brown, as she leaned over to look down.

Seeing his chance, the king stepped behind her. He pushed Autumn Brown into the ravine, then hurried home, rubbing his hands with glee.

When the weaver girls returned in the evening, and found the house empty, they were worried. So they went out in search of their new companion. Suddenly, they heard someone calling from far away in the woods. They followed the voice and what did they find? Autumn Brown, shouting for help from deep down in the ravine! They pulled her out and hastened home.

Back at the house, Autumn Brown told them what had happened.

"That hunter must have been the king," said the weaver girls, and they made her promise to stay in the house if she didn't want to go with them to town.

Meanwhile the king had reached the palace. He ran to the mirror.

"Mirror, mirror, bright and clear!
Show me she's dead! Make her appear!"

The mirror replied:

"The princess is nowhere to be seen.

Her friends pulled her out of the ravine."

The king saw red. In his great rage, he thought up a new plan. He disguised himself as a woodcutter and, taking a long rope with him, set off once again.

Autumn Brown was once more alone in the house. The weaver girls had gone to the town to buy yarn, but before they left, they had made Autumn Brown promise not to open the door to anyone.

Autumn Brown was carving a wooden plate when there came a knock at the door.

"Good ladies, help me please!" the king called through the door.

Autumn Brown looked out of the window and called, "Go away! Find someone else to help you."

But the king, whom Autumn Brown had not recognised, persisted. "I have no wood to build a house for my wife and children."

Autumn Brown felt sorry for the man. *He's just a poor woodcutter,* she thought to herself, and stepped outside. "Show me where we need to go and I'll help you," she said to the king, smiling.

The king led the way, and they walked and walked until they reached the middle of the woods, where a huge oak tree stood.

"Help me to measure it, so I can see if it will do," the king requested.

He gave Autumn Brown one end of the rope, pretending that he was using it to measure the width of the tree. He took it once around the great trunk, then twice, every time winding it around Autumn Brown too, and keeping on until he ran out of rope. Autumn Brown struggled and shouted, but the king left her there, to be torn to pieces by the wolves.

Luckily, the weaver girls were anxious about leaving Autumn Brown alone, so they did not spend long in town.

When they got home and found that she was nowhere to be seen, they knew that the king had visited again. They went into the woods, and soon found Autumn Brown tied to the tree with the wolves already circling her. They quickly untied her and they all ran home.

Back at the house, Autumn Brown told them what had happened.

"That was the king! Why did you go with him? Make sure you don't leave the house again or, you'll see, there'll come a time when we won't be able to save you," said the weaver girls.

Autumn Brown promised not to leave the house, and the next time the weaver girls went to market, she locked the door carefully.

As soon as the king got back to the palace, he ran to the mirror:

"Mirror, mirror, bright and clear!
Show me she's dead, so I can jeer!"

The mirror replied:

"Autumn Brown lives deep in the wood.
With the weaver girls her life is good,"

The king was now very angry indeed. He got his cook to roast a rabbit and he placed poison inside it. Then, once again, he disguised himself as a huntsman and went off into the woods. When he reached the weaver girls' house, he knocked at the door.

"Go away! I'm not letting you in," shouted Autumn Brown.

"I don't want to come in. That's not why I'm here. I've shot a rabbit and roasted it, and I thought I would share it with whoever lives in this house," said the king.

Warily, Autumn Brown looked out of the window. Then she said, "No, thank you. I can't accept it."

"Maybe you think it's poisoned?" laughed the king. "Watch then. I'll break it in half. I'll eat the left leg and you can eat the right."

That was all very well, but the wicked king had put the poison in the rabbit's right leg, and when Autumn Brown took it from him and bit into it, she fell to the ground, dead.

"Let those weaver girls try to save her now!" said the king, pleased with himself.

When he got back to the palace, he asked the mirror:

"Mirror, mirror, bright and clear!
Show me the weaver girls in tears!"

The mirror showed him the weaver girls rolling up to the door of their house on their cart. They went inside and, seeing Autumn Brown lying on the floor, knew right away what had happened. They picked her up and laid her on a bed, but Autumn Brown did not wake up.

"She's dead! She's dead!"

The weaver girls wept and wailed, their hearts almost breaking with grief. With great sorrow, they wove a beautiful dress for her, and when they had clothed her in it, all seven of them gathered around her and sobbed bitterly for three days and three nights.

Then they wiped their eyes and said to each other, "Autumn Brown will not lie in the dark earth. We will have a glass coffin made for her, so we can look at her always."

This they did, and when the coffin was ready, they laid her inside and had her name engraved upon it, adding that she had been the daughter of a king. They took the coffin up to the top of a hill and set it down in a clearing. From that day forward, one of the weaver girls was always standing guard over it. The creatures of the wood also came to weep over Autumn Brown's body.

Time passed, but Autumn Brown did not change. Her skin remained as brown as autumn leaves, and her dark hair shone. She looked as if she were asleep.

One day a prince from a neighbouring kingdom rode into the woods to hunt. He came upon the coffin on top of the hill and stopped to read the inscription.

What a beautiful girl! he thought as he gazed, transfixed, at Autumn Brown.

Eventually, he said to the weaver girls, "Sell me this coffin, and I will give you whatever you want in return."

The girls protested, saying they wouldn't sell Autumn Brown for the world. The prince, however, felt he couldn't bear to live even a day without being able to see her.

"Then give her to me," begged the prince.

The weaver girls took pity on him and made him a present of the coffin. The prince called his servants, told them to carry the coffin, and off they set. They walked and walked, until one of the servants stumbled. As the coffin jolted, the morsel of poisoned meat fell out of Autumn Brown's mouth and, miracle of miracles, she opened her eyes!

"Where am I?" she asked.

"With me," said the prince and told her everything that

had happened. Then he said, "Come home with me and be my wife."

"So I will!" replied Autumn Brown. "I'll gladly be yours."

And that is what happened. The prince himself lifted her onto his horse. They galloped home and sent out the news that the prince was going to be married.

Guests came to the wedding from far and wide, so many that there was barely room for them all in the palace. The wicked king was also invited. He put on his finest clothes, but before he left, he sat down before the mirror.

"Mirror, mirror, bright and clear!
Show me the prince's bride so dear!"

The mirror showed him Autumn Brown, who was busy pinning up her hair.

"Mirror, mirror, smudged and smeared!
Autumn Brown's dead. She can't be here?!"

cried the king in horror.

"Autumn Brown is alive – alive!
With the prince she'll surely thrive,"

answered the mirror.

When the king heard these words, his face turned purple, and he fell to the ground. He never got up again.

Autumn Brown married the prince and became a good queen to her new country. And for all we know, she may still be living there happily today.

István Lakatos

The Witch's Tale

For years the cradle had stood there, the one in which the rats had eaten her son. She had avoided that corner of the cottage ever since. Why hadn't she removed the cradle? Even she didn't know. Perhaps it was her never-ending grief. Or perhaps the cradle was a reminder of how alone she was. And how alone she would always be.

Everyone thought she was a witch, but she didn't care. At least they left her in peace. People were afraid of her because she lived alone in the middle of the forest. But they liked her baking well enough – even if they would never admit it. On market days the witch would sell gingerbread biscuits, meringues, crescent-shaped walnut biscuits dusted with icing sugar, crumbly, savoury *pogácsas* and chocolate cake. Once, she had been a skilled pastry chef and she had loved her work. When her son died, her passion for baking had faded away, but it was the only thing she could do to keep herself busy. And it brought in a pretty penny, of course.

At the market, the witch's stall was always piled high with good things to eat, and the customers would crowd around it, pretending they were just looking. When a person reached the front of the queue, they would simply jab a finger at whatever they wanted, throw down the right money, and be gone. Not a word would pass between the witch and her customers. Every now and then, a grubby child would pocket a biscuit or two, but the witch didn't mind. She was pleased when she could make a child happy.

On the day the two children came creeping round her cottage, the witch was baking. She had put a few baskets of gingerbread biscuits in various shapes out on the windowsill to cool and was busy with the next batch when she happened to look up and spot them. The boy was stuffing iced dragons, crescent moons and smart hussars on horseback into his mouth, three at a time. He looked about five years old, and his face was dirty. Behind him, an older girl, maybe twelve, was pacing up and down and telling the boy to hurry up, that she had a bad feeling about this place.

The witch opened the door and invited the children in. The girl didn't want to enter the cottage, but the little boy, who was sniffing the air and gazing at the cakes and biscuits spread all over the table, barged in without a word. The girl called after him, but as he ignored her, she unwillingly followed him in, grumbling as she went. She glanced around the room suspiciously, then looked the witch up and down, but the boy was already explaining, through a mouth full of cake, how they didn't get enough to eat at home, how their parents had put them out in the forest and told them to go off by themselves because they could no longer feed them. To find their way back, the children had secretly scattered breadcrumbs behind them. But when their parents had gone and the children wanted to set off for home, there were no crumbs to be seen. The birds had eaten them all up. The girl shrugged her shoulders listlessly. There were dark circles under her eyes.

A fine story! Breadcrumbs, night drawing on . . . Were the children really that stupid? They didn't even have a lamp! They must have been stumbling about in the dark for a long time before the light in the cottage windows led them to her. The witch was far from convinced that their parents had tried to get rid of them. There had probably been an argument at home, and the girl, as was common with children of her age, had gone off in a huff, to teach her parents a lesson. She had grabbed her little brother and off they'd run.

The little boy was enjoying himself. Imagine! Her own son might have grown up to be a boy like this one: a little kid with hair as black as pitch and sparkling eyes, and perhaps he would have stuffed himself with biscuits in the same way, grinning like a jack-o'-lantern. The girl was eating quietly, her head tucked down into her shoulders, her eyes darting here and there, like an animal trapped in a corner.

As she watched the little boy, eating and eating and beaming with delight, the witch began to feel happy, like she had long ago when there had been a baby cooing and laughing in the cradle.

It was getting late though, time to get to bed. The girl protested, but in the middle of the forest, at the dead of night, where else could they go? The witch laid a rug on the floor for the girl and gave her a pillow and a blanket. The little boy she put to bed in the cradle. It was a big one and he fitted into it comfortably.

The children were exhausted from their wanderings in the forest and soon fell asleep. Before she lay down, the girl gave her brother a kiss. She was reassured to know he would be close to her all night. After a little while, she fell into an uneasy sleep in which she muttered and ground her teeth.

The witch sat for a short time by the cradle, looking at the boy. Then she remembered the rats. What if they crept out from somewhere? A little child like this one wouldn't stand a chance. The witch decided to sit by the cradle and keep watch through the night. She gazed and gazed at the little boy, wishing he was hers.

At dawn, as always, the witch started her daily chores. She was unsteady on her feet and could barely keep her eyes open, but she didn't regret her vigil. She was no longer alone. Here was the little boy, and finally there would be meaning to her day. For once, it wasn't only the household chores driving her on, but a desire to make this day a special one for the children. For the little boy.

She fetched water from the well and started to prepare breakfast. She couldn't remember when she had last smiled this much – or when she had last smiled at all for that matter. Perhaps it had been when another small body was still breathing softly in the cradle.

Both children ate well. The little boy gobbled up his food, almost forgetting to swallow, and got jam everywhere, even in his hair. The girl was no longer quite so mistrustful as she had been the previous evening. Although she didn't eat much, she ate more confidently and didn't sit hunched over the table as if sensing some great danger around her.

Why was she so afraid anyway? The witch didn't want to hurt anyone. She was glad to have the children at her house!

When they had finished, the girl helped to clear the table and wash up. Then she asked what was going to happen next.

The witch chewed on a buttery *kifli* and looked thoughtfully at the freckled, red-haired girl. The girl was afraid because she

didn't know what was going to become of her and her brother. Maybe they really had been sent away from home.

The witch asked the children if they wanted to stay. She was happy to have them, she said, after living so long by herself. She didn't tell them about her dead son, of course, why would she? The girl cast her eyes down and said nothing. The little boy paid no attention, continuing to stuff himself with food and play with the cutlery. He banged down a plate a little more roughly than he should have, and it broke into pieces.

Never mind. I can sweep it up, thought the witch.

She had a new family now; that was all she could think about. The witch smiled.

All through lunch, the little boy appeared to be turning something over in his mind. As he chewed, his head went up and down. Then he put down his spoon, leaned his elbows on the table, rested his chin on his hands and put a question to the witch. Could they invite their mother and father to her house? Their parents were hungry too, and they were very good people. The lady would like them. And it was really nice here, he said, because he could eat lots of tasty things, but now he wanted to go home.

The witch looked at the girl. At first she frowned at her little brother, then she went red. She glanced at the witch uneasily, before giving a little nod. Their parents really were hungry. And they really were good people. And whatever had happened, she and her brother belonged at home.

"Tomorrow," said the witch. She added that today she had only cooked for three. But tomorrow she would light the stove and the oven; she would use sackfuls of flour, sugar and walnuts and she would take the best *kolbász* smoked sausages down off the hooks in the ceiling. She would prepare such a feast, and afterwards the children and their parents would be able to take home as much food as they could carry.

The children nodded. So delighted was the little boy that
he jumped up from his seat and started racing around the
table, whooping. He didn't stop till evening. He knocked down
a few things, of course, but everything could be swept up.

That evening, the witch sat for a long time by the cradle.
She listened to the little boy's breathing and his little
snuffles, and all she could think about was how the next
day the cradle would once again be empty and that no one
would ever sleep in it again.

Then she gave a start. When she realised that she had
dropped off, she was horrified. No harm had come to the
little boy, thank goodness, but the witch was terrified of the
rats. They must not come near this boy! She wondered what
she ought to do, then finally she brought in an old rabbit
cage. She cleaned it thoroughly, then wound thick wire
around it so that the rats would be unable to squeeze
between the bars. Gently, she lifted the child out of the
cradle and placed him in the cage. Then, on a sudden
impulse, she dug out the old teddy bear she had once sewed
for her son. It was dirty and a little moth-eaten, but when
she laid it next to the little boy, he hugged it to him as if it
had always been his own.

The witch lay down, but she couldn't fall asleep. She was
scared of the day to come. Scared of losing the children. Yes,
the girl too. She didn't want to be alone any more. Gradually,
she cried herself to sleep.

In the middle of the night, the boy woke and looked
around, startled. Although it was dark, he could see enough
to know that he wasn't lying in the cradle, and that
something cold and threatening was surrounding him. He
whimpered at first, then cried out in fear. The witch woke
up instantly and leapt towards the cage. Taking the boy,
she held him close and hushed him, keeping one eye on his
sleeping sister all the while. She, too, had been startled
awake. The witch told her the boy had had a bad dream,

and she hoped that the girl wouldn't notice the cage. She wouldn't understand. She would think that the witch wanted to lock her brother up.

When the little boy and the girl had both settled down and were sleeping again, the witch placed the boy in the cradle. She couldn't put him back in the cage after what had happened. Instead, she sat down beside him and watched over him for the rest of the night.

When it grew light, the witch got to work – but not before she had pushed the cage against the wall and covered it with a rug. True to her word, she lit both the stove and the oven, brought sacks of flour, sugar, walnuts and other ingredients from the pantry and laid out the *kolbász* sausages and bacon. She kneaded dough for the bread, plucked a chicken and picked vegetables from the little garden behind the cottage.

When the children had woken up, the girl helped with the work. The little boy dashed up and down, whooping and shouting and eating all the while. How wonderful that he would see his parents again and that they would have full stomachs too, he cried. The girl worked quietly. Sneaking a glance at the witch, the girl saw that she had stopped stirring the pot, and that her whole body seemed to have deflated, as if, in the space of a moment, she had shrivelled up. She looked over at her brother, then at the cradle standing in the dark corner, and suddenly, she understood everything.

She put her arms around the witch.

Then the two of them worked on in silence, while the little boy continued to whoop and shout.

It was well into the afternoon by the time everything was ready. They had eaten only a modest lunch, so as to have an appetite when it was time for the feast. As they finished their work, the witch asked the girl if she would go home and fetch her parents. The girl hesitated a moment, then

nodded. Everything would be all right. The witch told her in
great detail how to find her way back to the house, and as a
token of her good intentions, and to show the children's
parents she meant well, she packed a basket of food for the
girl to take with her, filling it with as many good things the
girl was able to carry.

All the witch asked was that the little boy be allowed to
stay with her until the family returned.

The girl agreed and then set off with the basket.

The boy and the witch were left alone.

The witch stood and looked at him. She didn't dare ask
him the question that was on her mind. Even though
everything was ready to welcome the children's parents, she
began to make another batch of biscuits. She had to keep
herself busy somehow, and maybe while she worked, she
would manage to pluck up the courage. Perhaps if she did
what she was good at – and not just good but the best for
miles around – then she would recognise something she had
a tendency to forget: that she was worth something; that
she, too, was entitled to a life that was complete.

Hours went by and evening drew on. The witch tried to
pull herself together. Now, she felt, was the time. But she
was trembling. She couldn't look the little boy in the eye.
She went over to the oven to put more wood on the fire.
Bent over in front of the dancing flames, she looked back at
the boy, and finally dared, timidly, to ask her question.

"Wouldn't you prefer to stay here . . . with me?"

The little boy was still dashing around the room, and he
didn't stop at her words. Perhaps he hadn't even heard
them. The witch was shaking from top to toe. She couldn't
straighten up.

"Wouldn't you prefer to stay here with me?" she asked
again, louder this time.

The little boy skidded to a halt.

"To live here with me in this cottage and eat delicious

cakes and biscuits every day?"

The little boy frowned and looked at the witch, puzzled.

"Let me be your mother," the witch pleaded.

"But I've got a mother," replied the boy.

The witch looked sideways at the rabbit cage. "I could lock you up in that cage," she said. "You'll stay here if I want you to."

"Don't you dare touch my son!" roared a powerful male voice behind her.

The children's parents were standing in the doorway, the girl behind them, hanging her head.

The witch was startled, but not cowed. She straightened up. "I won't be spoken to like that by someone who threw his children out into the forest so they would starve to death."

She didn't even raise her voice.

The father was trembling with rage. His wife, a thin, pale woman, touched her husband's arm and said quietly, "Let's go."

The man grabbed his son and, towering over the witch, he hissed, "If I ever see you near my children again, I will burn down your house with you inside it!"

With that, he dragged his son out of the cottage. The little boy was so frightened, he didn't make a sound.

The children's mother followed them, but the girl stood for a moment in the doorway and whispered, so softly it could barely be heard, "He's a good man, really."

With that, she turned on her heel and walked off into the darkness.

The witch stood there, helpless and angry. She wanted to run after them and snatch the children back. But she knew she would stand no chance. Would the parents throw their children out into the forest again? Or would the man decide to prove her wrong, and try harder to feed them from now on? Was there even any truth to what the children had told her? Now, once again, the witch wasn't so certain. She was

so furious, she felt like killing the man.

She looked over at the table, which was groaning with the weight of roast meats, cakes, fresh bread and *pogácsas*. She looked at the *kolbász* sausages and the side of bacon. If it wasn't to be, it wasn't to be. She sat down and started to eat. She didn't look at what she was eating. It had no taste for her. She let the mounting rage within her direct her whirling thoughts.

She remembered how the biscuits left to cool on the windowsill had lured the little boy to her in the first place.

Then the witch smiled. That's how it would be from now on, then. And she would make good use of the cage too . . .

She got up and put the cakes, biscuits and *pogácsas* out on the windowsill. Then she began to make more gingerbread biscuits. She would decorate the whole house with them, let the aroma of gingerbread waft on the breeze for miles around!

More children would come to her house.

And she would make sure they stayed.

Judit B. Tóth

The Ice King

Mammoth and Mug lived on the Grumbly housing estate, on the first floor of one of its many tower blocks. Their flat was tiny. Mammoth, however, was large, both up and down and from side to side, and soft as can be. On cold winter days, it was especially nice to snuggle up with her.

It was Mammoth who had given her blonde, blue-eyed girlfriend the name Mug. Mug was a small, fragile girl and she liked it when Mammoth took her by the hand. It made her feel warm. Mug was very often in tears. She cried if the thread broke when she was sewing a doll. She cried when she saw the news on TV, and she cried like a small child if she bumped into something and hurt herself. When this happened, Mammoth would pull Mug to her and give her a long, soft, comforting hug.

Mammoth liked to bake cheesecakes: huge, round, snow-white cakes. Everyone on the housing estate was a customer of hers. Word of her baking talents even spread beyond the estate. On Sundays, it wasn't only the nursery school children who would beg their parents to buy a cake from Mammoth; it was the bigger boys and girls too.

For those who didn't like cheesecake, Mammoth would make a marzipan cake, with a real marzipan forest on top, or a fruit tart with big, glossy strawberries. And secretly, Mammoth would give out free cakes to the parents of the poorer children. Her hot oven purred away in the little flat, warming it through, and in the afternoons, the rooms were filled with honey-sweet aromas. These mouth-watering

smells even filtered into the stair-well.

While Mammoth was baking, Mug would go out to the playground and sit on her favourite purple bench. Children would gather around her, eager to see what kind of doll she was sewing that day. Mug made her dolls from rags, and these dolls, believe it or not, came to life in the children's hands. One doll would blink slowly as if it had woken up from a long sleep. Another would snuggle up to its new owner as if it had found its long-lost mother. Mug's dolls sneezed and coughed just like real children. A few of them were decidedly cheeky, sticking out their tongues at their young owners and some were even known to fart!

Winter arrived. Everyone on the Grumbly estate grumbled and grouched about the cold. It went right through you, freezing you to the bone. Mammoth and Mug stayed at home as much as they could. Mammoth had a feeling that this winter was going to be a long one, maybe so long it would have no end.

Christmas came, but it was different from usual. The weather was so cold that the hot water circulating in the building froze in the pipes before it could warm their flat through. Mammoth baked her cheesecakes, but their flat was still cold. Deep snow made it difficult to walk in the streets, so Mammoth and Mug were unable to get themselves a Christmas tree. Mammoth found a little bottle of pine-scented oil, which they sniffed at, shivering.

Time went by and Easter came around, but winter was still with them. It grew even colder. The nights were longer and the days shorter. Nobody felt like going to their friends' houses for the Easter custom of *locsolkodás*, where women and girls would be sprinkled with water or cologne, and they certainly didn't fancy getting wet. The sky was cloudy and grey, the pavements were covered in ice, and so were the bare branches of the trees.

When she woke up one chilly summer's morning, Mug saw a frost flower on the window. It wasn't like the other frost flowers. It was brighter and more beautiful. Mug remembered that she had seen one like it in her dreams. The frost flower glittered purple and blue – invitingly, it seemed to Mug – and it grew brighter and brighter.

Outside, the wind was howling and tossing the trees about. It occurred to Mug that the pantry was empty and the fridge was bare except for a few *túrórudis* – cream cheese bars covered in chocolate. She jumped out of bed and set off for the shop to get bread and cream cheese.

As she walked along, all Mug could think of was the frost flower. She felt as if someone had sent it to her, but she didn't know who. Her heart shrank, and she felt more afraid than usual.

The shop was quiet and cold. When Mug had filled her bag with bread, butter and cream cheese, she set off home to have breakfast with Mammoth. However, when she turned the corner, she heard a terrible rushing noise. There was

a blinding whiteness all around her, then – *whoosh!* – the snowstorm sucked her in, so roughly that she couldn't move. Her bag fell into the snow, with the bread, the butter and the cream cheese inside it, while the wind buffeted and dragged at Mug, lifting her into the air. She cried and sobbed, but could do nothing to save herself. The wind carried her higher and higher.

The dirty white tower blocks of the Grumbly estate grew smaller and smaller. Mug could still make out a smudge of red – which was the swings in the playground – before this too disappeared. Below her, she saw nothing but bands of greeny-grey, bluey-grey and yellowy-grey. She was very cold. Darkness came and covered the Earth. Only the beckoning white disc of the Moon was visible, and the stars.

Then Mug caught sight of a bright city in the sky, far away. The wind was carrying her straight up to the courtyard of the Ice King's palace.

Mug had never seen so many towers. They were white and blue with sparkling, arched windows. The palace was scary, and something was missing from it – not only from the palace, but from everywhere around it. Mug soon realised that it didn't matter which way she looked, she couldn't see even a scrap of shadow.

As Mug entered the palace, she saw its walls were made of ice. Something was drawing her further and further in. She walked along a wide, empty corridor and then found herself in an enormous hall. In the centre of the hall, a stern-faced man with a moustache of hoar frost was painting a picture of some kind. He wore a crown of diamonds on his blond head.

"I've been expecting you," said the Ice King, smiling at Mug.

"Are you a painter?" asked Mug.

"I am the Painter of Ice," said the king. "Whatever I paint turns to ice and becomes part of my empire."

The Ice King pulled Mug to him and planted an ice-cold

kiss on her forehead. Mug felt the cold slowly penetrate to her heart. She felt light, as if she could fly, and was no longer afraid.

"Are you cold?" asked the Ice King.

"Not at all!" laughed Mug. "I can't feel anything. I'm not even afraid. I feel as if all pain and sorrow has left my heart. It's like, I don't know, falling asleep in the snow."

Back at home, meanwhile, Mammoth was waiting and waiting for Mug to come back. She paced up and down the flat, unable to settle to anything. Their little place somehow seemed cavernous and untidy. At every turn, she stumbled over her girlfriend's dolls. They sat on the bed, propped up against the wall, and there was even one lying on its tummy on top of the wardrobe.

Hours went by and evening drew on. Mammoth couldn't imagine why Mug hadn't come home. She called everyone she could think of: Mug's mother, her friends, her rabbi, but no one had any idea where she could be. Mammoth called the police, but they told her that if someone had only been gone for half a day, they didn't consider them a missing person.

Mammoth remembered the snowstorm that morning. *Maybe Mug's in trouble,* she thought, horrified. *Maybe this endless winter has swallowed her up.*

She turned off the light and looked out of the window. The clouds had gone. The moon and the stars shone as brightly as jewels cast onto the night sky.

Mammoth put the *túrórudis* in her canvas bag and pulled on her blue sweater, then the red one, then the white one too. She struggled into her quilted coat, then set off to search for Mug.

Outside it was horribly cold, much colder than it had been the day before or the day before that. It seemed to Mammoth that the sky was a shade darker too. The stars seemed further away from each other. The moon and the

stars were less bright, and even the streetlights had gone
out. The windows of the Grumbly estate had gone dark too,
and black night descended on Mammoth.

She felt her way along, slipping on the hard, frozen snow.
It was very still. The only sounds were her footsteps as she
trudged along, and the miaowing of a hungry cat.

Mammoth was exhausted. She had been walking for
hours in the pitch black. Her phone had stopped working
and she couldn't see her watch. She felt, all of a sudden, that
time had ceased to be. There were no minutes or hours, only
the pitch-black darkness. She grew sleepy, and wanted
simply to fall into the snow and sleep and sleep.

Then, however, she heard noises, someone humming and
the clatter of pans.

"Come on in, if you're cold," said a man with an unusually
deep voice.

Mammoth shuffled in, out of the dark, into the dark.
She sensed only that, inside, the cold was less cruel.

"Welcome to my home," Mammoth heard the kind, deep
voice say. "I built it out of cardboard boxes. I lost my flat
a long time ago. Have some of my soup, then lie down on
one of my quilts and sleep for a bit."

Mammoth sipped at the soup, then lay down on the
musty quilt, pulled her coat up to her nose, and slept.
In her dream, she was very cold. She dreamed that Mug
was weeping over the stories in the news and that she was
comforting her. The dream warmed Mammoth up. It was
good to feel Mug's face against hers.

When she woke up, it was still dark.

"We're living through the Dark Days," said the man who
lived in the cardboard box. "The Endless Winter."

"Do you know where Mug is?" Mammoth asked him.

"I know you're looking for your girlfriend," replied the
man. "The birds are singing about it and the trees are
whispering about it. If you think hard about Mug, you'll

find her, but if I were you, I'd go home without her."

The man fell silent. Mammoth asked more questions but he would say nothing further.

As Mammoth stepped out of the cardboard-box house, she thought hard about Mug and the dream she had had. She thought about their faces touching.

Suddenly, a howling wind started up. It shook Mammoth about, then – *whoosh!* – it lifted her into the air. A hazelnut *túrórudi* fell out of her bag, then another, and a walnut one too. Mammoth flew and flew in the icy, pitch-black darkness, thinking all the time about Mug. She had the feeling that the darkness was deepening, the sky getting even blacker.

Warm, black colours are all around me, she told herself, her teeth chattering. *Bone-black, seed-black, grape-black.*

A frost flower was glinting up ahead. Mammoth wasn't sure if she was dreaming. It was soaring and leaping in the air. Towers and blueish onion domes began to glimmer in the distance, then the sky was flooded with a blinding light and Mammoth found herself in the Ice King's courtyard.

A spotless, white palace towered in front of her. Mammoth looked in at one of the windows and was amazed to find that it wasn't made of glass but was woven from thousands of frost flowers. Mammoth, too, thought it odd that there were no shadows in this place.

She went in through the gate and came face to face with Mug.

Or rather, not Mug, but a picture of her.

Mug was beautiful in the painting. Her eyes were a brighter blue than of old and, as they gazed off into space, they were merry and calm in a way that Mammoth didn't remember. She wanted to stroke the picture but thought better of it.

A clerk in a blue uniform dashed past her, holding a great pile of folders and files. The small man let out a sneeze,

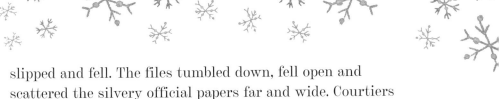

slipped and fell. The files tumbled down, fell open and
scattered the silvery official papers far and wide. Courtiers
and clerks came and went along the corridor, but no one
offered to help the little man. One of them even trod on
an important-looking document.

In the end, it was Mammoth who helped him gather up
the scattered papers. As she did so, she asked him how she
could find the girl in the painting.

The little man began to sneeze again, each sneeze louder
than the next until the palace shook with the sound.

"It's just my nerves," explained the little man. "How can
you ask such a thing? No one can gain access to the queen
just like that. She is the Ice King's wife. And her name is
Bimbinella, by the way."

"And why are there no shadows here?" asked Mammoth.

"Because that would remind us of our mortality," replied
the man. "Here, everything goes on for ever. I am forever
young, like Bimbinella. You, on the other hand, have crow's
feet at the corners of your eyes."

"Maybe I do. But I helped you," said Mammoth, crossly.

"That's true," mused the little man. "It's not customary
to help others around here."

He blew his nose into an enormous silk handkerchief.
"Now, what should we do about you, young lady? What
indeed? The truth is, you'd have to talk to three hundred
clerks, one after the other, and convince them you were
worthy to see Bimbinella before they would let you
anywhere near her. But why are you so set upon it?"

"Because . . . because I respect her," said Mammoth,
cunningly. "And because I have something to say which is
for her ears only."

The little man pulled at his ear lobe. "I'll tell the chief
clerk that you helped me. He can give you a pass with
a stamp on it that will get you in to see Bimbinella."

And so it turned out. The very same day, Mammoth was

admitted into the heart of the palace, Bimbinella's great
hall. Two rows of columns led to the dais where the queen
was sitting, surrounded by ladies-in-waiting, who stood
around her like lifeless dolls. Mammoth ran to her
girlfriend. She wanted to hug her, but Bimbinella pushed
her away with a shriek.

"How dare you!" she said. "You're no more than a beggar
off the streets! How on earth did you get gain admittance to
my chamber in rags such as these?"

"But . . . don't you know me?" asked Mammoth. "I've had
such a long, difficult journey to find you."

Bimbinella narrowed her bright blue eyes. They flashed
at Mammoth. "I have no idea who you are. My friends are
queens and consorts. They are the only people I talk to,
and then only by telephone."

"But it's me, Mammoth!" said her girlfriend, stammering
in her desperation.

"What exactly is it you want? Spit it out, will you?"
shouted Bimbinella. "I don't have time for this!"

Mammoth was trying not to cry. Her voice wobbled.
"Have you forgotten our little flat on the estate, where
you sewed dolls for the children? Don't you remember
my cheesecakes?"

"You're not making any sense!" cut in Bimbinella, in a
voice Mammoth didn't recognise. "I never want to see you
again. You had better not cross the threshold of my chamber
ever again."

Mammoth burst into tears and, as one hot tear dropped
onto Bimbinella's hand, life sprang like a flame into the
queen's eyes. She was astonished to find warmth spreading
through her body. Suddenly, she remembered their little flat
on the Grumbly estate, and how lovely it had been to
snuggle up close to Mammoth on cold winter days. She was
no longer Bimbinella, but once again sweet, timid Mug. She
stepped over to Mammoth and awkwardly pulled her close,

sinking into her big, soft embrace.

"Let's go home," she whispered, and they wasted no time in doing so. They ran out of the palace. No more shuffling or trudging. They ran as fast as if they were being carried along by the wind.

The army of little clerks was left far behind.

"Hey there, Mammoth!" boomed a male voice from among the snowdrifts.

It was the man who lived in the cardboard-box house. He waved cheerily at Mammoth and Mug. "Here's a piece of my paper palace. You'll get home faster with this!"

Mammoth and Mug jumped onto the piece of cardboard, and as they slid onwards, they found themselves faced by a blinding snowstorm. There was no way around it. With a *whoosh*, the wind snatched them up. The shards of ice in the air seemed to laugh merrily, then suddenly Mammoth and Mug found themselves back in the Grumbly estate.

When they got into their little flat, Mug lay down on the bed among her sleeping dolls and Mammoth stretched out next to her. They pulled the quilt over themselves and fell fast asleep.

The next day they woke to find the sun shining in through the window onto their faces. The frost flowers had melted off the windowpanes, and spring had arrived.

Andrea Tompa

Iron Imi

To E, with thanks

Once upon a time, out beyond the end of the village, where the poorest people lived – further out even, where the land was stony and the marshes began – there lived a poor man and his poor wife.

The old couple passed their days together, leaning on each other like two sacks of potatoes, with nothing more to their names than the leaky roof over their heads. Though they had worked hard all their lives, they had always bent their backs over someone else's fields. The Lord God had not granted them land of their own, nor even a child. The frosts and the winter wind cared nothing for the poor. The icy blast just blew and blew, in through the cracks in the walls.

One day, when they were setting off for the forest once again to gather a few sticks to make a fire, the old woman sighed. "How much longer must we cart this wretched life about on our backs? We've nothing to call our own, and we're too old to hope the Almighty will give us a child."

The old man went on ahead, treading a path through the deep snow for his wife, for all they had, in their great poverty, was their love for each other.

"Now then, wife," he replied. "That's enough of that. It's not our place to hold the Lord to account, here on Earth. We've no business doing it."

"Then what *is* our business, I'd like to know?" said the old woman dejectedly as she walked through the snow in her husband's footsteps.

When they got to the forest, they saw that the snow was so thick it had buried all the fallen branches. They cast around but could see nothing but the big, bare trees and the deep snow.

Then the man noticed some fresh tracks. Someone had been along in small boots, leaving their prints behind them. "We're too late, wife. Someone's been here already and collected up all the branches."

"A woman, I'd say," replied his wife, looking at how small the prints were. "Let's move on and hope for better luck elsewhere."

The old man and his wife were turning for home when all of a sudden, they heard a thin, mewling sound. They stopped and listened. Was it an animal caught in a trap?

They followed the sound deeper into the forest. When they got closer, they looked all around, but couldn't see where it was coming from.

The mewling went on and on.

"What can it be, husband?"

"A fox, maybe, caught in a trap," replied the old man.

"That's no fox, husband. That's a human. I may be old and doddery, but I know a child's voice when I hear it."

They searched all around under the trees. Then the old woman looked up, for the sound seemed to her to be coming from right over her head. Well, what should she see but a large, richly embroidered shawl hanging from a branch!

"Come quickly, husband. Look, there! What's that, up in the tree?" she said.

The old man grabbed the branch and saw that someone had tied the shawl tightly onto it. He bent the branch down and undid the knot. "Someone's gone and left their shawl here. A fancy one too. By the stitching, I'd say it belonged to a fine young lady."

He lifted down the shawl, and just then, the voice – which up till then had been mewling and whimpering – broke into

loud laughter. They unfolded the shawl, and what do you think they found inside it? Great Father Almighty, a tiny little child! The tiniest you ever saw!

"Mother! Father!" cried the little voice. The tiny child laughed and laughed and held out his little arms towards his parents. "Here you are at last!"

Well now, the two old people just stared and stared until the child cried out again.

"Don't you know me, Mother? Don't you know me, Father? It's me! I've arrived!"

At that, a smile broke over the old couple's faces, and they passed the child between them, gazing at him in wonder and turning him this way and that.

"Look at you! You're a blessing from God!" they kept saying to the child.

"Look, husband! Oh, look at our son!"

"Oh, wife! Here's our own sweet child!"

Tears coursed down their old cheeks like mountain streams in springtime. They wrapped the child tightly in the shawl, tucking the ends in to keep out the cold, and set off to carry him home.

As they went along through the snow, the wife said, "Husband, we haven't gathered so much as an armful of wood. Tell me, how am I going to cook for this child?"

The old man just scratched his head and said, "I'll take up the cellar steps. You can burn those, wife. There's nothing down there anyway, so we've no need for them."

And the child said, "Don't you worry about it, Mother! I'll run out to the edge of the village for wood, if you can just give me a nice mug of milk first."

"Now, where would I get that from, my boy, when we have nothing at all? We have a handful of *málé* to make porridge. I'll boil that up for you."

"Go and ask the neighbour for a mug of milk, Father. Tell them your wife's had a baby, but her milk hasn't come in yet."

"Oh, son! Our neighbour's the penny-pinching type. He won't give me any."

"Just go on over to his house, Father. He will."

When they got back home, the old man took an old, cracked mug round to the neighbour's house and told him a son had been born to him and his wife. The neighbour gave him a hard look, and said nothing, but the old man brought the mug home full of fresh milk. The child drank up every drop of the warm milk, then leapt up to fetch brushwood from the edge of the village. The old man said he would go along with him to show him the way, but the boy told his father not to bother. Instead, he told the old man to sweep out the range, so it would be ready to cook on when he returned.

What were they supposed to cook, wondered the old woman, when all they had was a handful of *málé*?

The boy ran off on his tiny legs, taking only an old, frayed rope to tie up the brushwood. The old man and his wife started to sweep out the firebox but were too busy rejoicing to work very hard. The old man had just swept out the last of the ash, when the boy came running back, red-cheeked. He had such an enormous bundle of sticks on his back that nothing of him could be seen. It was a wonder he could carry it!

"Here I am, Father," he said. "And I'm really hungry."

"Well, son, we'll get on and boil up that little bit of *málé* for you as fast as we can. We don't need any as we're old and can fill our stomachs with happiness as we look at our son."

The old woman filled a big pot with water and set it on the hot plate. They lit a fire underneath, and a moment later, it was giving off so much heat, they could only marvel. The woman brought out the handful of *málé* and sprinkled it into the pot. But as soon as she had poured it in, the pot was full to the brim. They all watched the huge potful of *málé* bubbling on the hot range. When it was ready, the old woman spooned out a helping for the boy, and there was enough for the old man and the old woman to have a big bowlful too. In the pot they found not only *málé*, but, wonder of wonders, there were thick pieces of fatty, fried bacon too! The lad ate one bowlful, then a second and a third.

Then the old woman asked him, "Have you had enough to eat, son?"

"Well, I wouldn't mind some more. Gathering wood is hungry work!"

"Help yourself then, son, and may it do you good!"

The boy ate seven bowls of *málé* and washed them down with seven buckets of water.

Then he lay down on the bricks at the top of the range and told his parents to wake him up early in the morning because he had work to do. The roof needed mending and so did the walls. But first, his parents should tell him a story to help him sleep.

The old couple started to tell him about their lives, and how they had always hoped to have a child. They sat down in front of the range and kept putting more sticks on the fire so it would burn good and hot. But the pile of sticks by the side of the range got no smaller. They sat and watched the little lad, who had started to snore so loudly it made the roof of the house tremble.

In the morning, the boy got up. He was so very, very small that his parents stared at him all over again. The lad was no bigger than a man's thumb, but when water had to be fetched from the well, he came back with two full buckets, balancing each one on a single finger. For breakfast, he ate seven whole bowls of *málé*, and asked for coffee to go with it.

"Coffee at your age, my son?"

"I'd like some coffee, yes, Father. Please give me some."

"We haven't got any coffee, my boy. We're poor people. You chose the wrong place to be born, coming into such a poor family."

"Maybe I did, but I'm not doing so badly. You'll see."

The little lad climbed up onto the kitchen table, and from there onto the cupboard, from where he pulled down a box. He opened it and a delicious smell drifted out.

"Mother, fancy you forgetting about this freshly ground coffee, when it smells so good! It was up here on top of the cupboard."

The old woman was amazed, because she hadn't tasted a drop of coffee since she was a young woman. They made a pot of good, strong black coffee and sat around the table like lords and ladies.

"Now then, Father. Let's fix up the sides of the house, seeing as there's plenty of us living in it. A fair few mice have made it their home too and there won't be space for us all before long!"

Well, the old man told him he didn't have a single tool, nor any boards to patch up the walls with.

"Go to the neighbour and ask for some, Father. Tell him

when your son is bigger, he'll pay him back."

Well, the old man went over to see the neighbour. The neighbour was astonished but gave the old man everything he asked for: nails, boards and the like.

The neighbour asked, "What's your son called, Imi?"

"Same as me. Imi. Iron Imi"

That was right, for when Iron Imi put his hands to something, it was done so fast, and done so well – so very well – that his poor parents could only stand and stare. Their eyes filled with tears to see how hard this little child of theirs was working.

When winter began to turn into spring, Iron Imi said that they should plant wheat and sweetcorn.

"But where would we plant it, son? We have no fields of our own."

"Here behind the house will be just fine, Father."

"That land's full of stones, son. The seeds won't take."

"Don't you worry about that, Father. We'll pick out the stones and use them to build a house so big, it'll make even the magistrate's jaw drop when he sees it."

Up he got, and started to clear the ground of stones and build a good, strong stone house with them. He told his father to ask the neighbour for a handful of wheat to sow in the ground, and to promise him that when his son grew up, he would pay the neighbour back.

With that, the old man went over to the neighbour's house again and asked him for a handful of wheat. The neighbour gave it to him. He also came down to the end of his garden to see how the little lad was working.

Well, Iron Imi worked as well as the best machine and as fast as the strongest digger. All he needed was seven buckets of water to drink and seven bowls of *málé* with good, fatty bacon to eat.

Iron Imi raised his hat to the neighbour and thanked him for the handful of wheat, which was already sending up green shoots tall enough to bend under the warm, spring wind. The neighbour went back into his house with a sour face, for his own wheat had barely stuck its nose out of the ground.

There was a marsh next to the village, and Iron Imi told his father to go to the magistrate and tell him he was going to drain it and use it for grazing his animals on.

"But what would we put out to graze there, son? We haven't so much as an old hen, let alone a pig or a goat."

"You can rest easy on that score, Father. We'll sell the wheat and get anything we want."

"Oh no, we won't, my boy! For once, we're going to put a loaf of white bread on our table!"

"There'll be so much wheat, Father, you won't be able to bring it all in."

And Iron Imi was right. There was so much wheat, they had to borrow the neighbour's cart to take it to market. They measured it out by the bushel, the old woman filling the basket while the old man counted the money. Iron Imi stood up on top of the pile of wheat and cried their wares. And however much they sold, there was still a great mountain of wheat in the cart.

Well, when they headed for home, they had so much money it wouldn't fit into the bushel basket, and the old woman had to take off her petticoat and carry the coins in that!

Iron Imi returned the cart to the neighbour full of wheat, and with a handful of gold. He thanked the neighbour and told him he would no longer be borrowing anything from him, as he was going to buy a cart, a pair of oxen, horses, pigs and everything they needed.

"But where will we put all these things, son?" the old man asked Iron Imi. "We don't even have a barn."

"We'll move into the stone house. Look, Mother, when I cleared the stones from the land behind our house, I used them to build a new house with thick, strong walls. They'll keep the house warm for you when you grow old."

"We're old already, my son! A house of stone is no good for us now. We're getting ready to go to another house, where we'll never feel the cold again."

"You're not old, Mother and Father! You haven't laid eyes on your grandchildren yet."

"Are you planning on giving us a grandchild too, my sweet boy?"

"I'd like a child as much as you, just I don't want to bring one into such poverty. Father, what did the magistrate say about the marsh?"

"He said it couldn't be drained."

"You just leave it to me, Father."

With that, Iron Imi went out to the marsh with two buckets. Before three days and three nights were up, he had drained it so well that only good, clean, black earth was left. He cut the reeds and tied them into bundles, then gave them to the poor to thatch their houses with. The water he carried to another spot, where he made a fishing lake. As soon as he had finished, the trout were leaping in it, so he brought seven buckets of fish home and fried them up for his parents. The old man and the old woman could only stand and stare in amazement. Never in all their born days had they eaten trout as delicious as the fish their son cooked for them.

When the magistrate heard that the poor man's son had planted a vegetable garden and an orchard on the spot where the marsh used to be, he went to see for himself. He saw how big the apples and pears were on the trees, and how the vines were bowed down with muscat grapes. Iron Imi was already collecting the grapes in barrels to make wine with.

The magistrate saw all this and flew into a rage. He said to Imi's father, "Now, listen here, my man. This marsh is common land. You must give it back."

"This is no marsh, your honour. It's good, rich farmland,

the like of which you've never seen!" said Iron Imi, stepping in front of his father.

The magistrate did not so much as glance at little Imi. Instead, he went on talking to his father. "You must give it back and that's that."

Well, the poor old man didn't know what to do. He told his son the land had to be returned.

"Cheer up, Father. I'll buy us another field."

With that, he plucked all the fruit, picked all the vegetables, chopped up all the trees, then flooded the land with the lake water.

"We'll give it back just as we got it. No one must be short-changed. We asked for a marsh, so that's what we'll give back. Call the magistrate over."

The magistrate came, and when he saw that he was getting a marsh rather than a beautiful garden, he went into a rage the likes of which you have never seen. Then he told the old man to call that little man over to him.

Iron Imi went over to the magistrate. "At your service, your honour. Nothing wrong with the marsh, I hope?"

"Listen here, you, whatever your name is! You listen to me!" The magistrate glared at Iron Imi and said, "I'll get you back for this."

And afterwards, the magistrate tried everything he could to punish Iron Imi, but nothing worked because Iron Imi made sure he couldn't be punished.

Iron Imi kept on working. He bought land and worked it, keeping a little of what he grew for his parents and himself, and selling the rest. He always left some crops in the fields for the poor to help themselves to. His favourite thing was plum jam, so he always kept a barrel of that. He now had two pairs of oxen and some pigs. As for his parents, whenever they looked at him, they never failed to wonder at the son they had been given, and gave thanks to the Almighty. They were so happy that they seemed quite young again.

One Sunday, when they were getting ready to go to church, the old woman said, "Imi, I thought I might wear that beautiful embroidered shawl we found you in."

All this time, they had taken great care of the shawl, keeping it mothballed and wrapped up in tissue paper. The old woman laid it across her shoulders and looked so young and beautiful in it, it was like a miracle!

They went to the church and sat themselves down at the back, in the poor people's pews. The magistrate arrived very late and was just coming into the church when he spotted the shawl. "Well now, woman, out with it! Where did you steal that shawl from?"

The old woman was alarmed. "We're not the stealing kind, your honour," she said.

"Then where did you get such a fine-looking shawl, I'd like to know?"

"We found it in the forest."

"And how exactly did you two come upon a shawl like that in the forest?"

The old woman was unwilling to tell him that the shawl wasn't all they had found, that there had been an even greater gift inside it.

The magistrate told her she would be punished for theft. The priest happened to be preaching about thieves, saying they would be punished when the Day of Judgement came, even though the priest himself had a reputation for stealing fruit from the village's most beautiful women.

When the old man and his wife came out of the church with Iron Imi, the magistrate was waiting for them. He said the old woman must go with him to the gaol, because she was a thief. The old woman burst out crying, tears streaming down her cheeks. She told her husband and child she'd rather go to gaol than tell the whole truth about the shawl.

Then Iron Imi stepped out in front of the magistrate, his hands on his hips and, when all the villagers had come out of the church, he said in a voice that could be heard half-way across the county (for the lad's voice was just as powerful as the rest of him), "My dear mother has never stolen a single shawl in the whole of her life."

The magistrate said she most certainly had stolen this shawl. He knew she had, because he knew who it belonged to. He himself had bought it at a fair to give to his maidservant.

"Well then, if it belonged to your honour's maidservant, your honour will also know what was inside it when my mother and father found it in the forest!"

"The girl's pretty, round shoulders, I should think – what else?" replied the magistrate, puffing and blowing and laughing in the little man's face.

"That's where you're wrong!" cried Iron Imi "In that shawl was my life!"

"What do you mean, your life?" said the magistrate, who, by that time, was staring at Iron Imi in amazement.

The maidservant in question happened to be standing right there beside the magistrate, and she had turned quite pale. She whispered, "Let it go, your honour. I don't mind about the shawl. I lost it when I was in the forest. It was a long time ago. Let it go. I've no need for it now. You gave me another one."

But the magistrate wouldn't let it go. He was too worked up.

Then Iron Imi said to him, "My dear mother came by the shawl honestly. She found it knotted to a tree in the forest and inside it she found a little child that she took care of and raised as her own. I am the child that she found in the shawl. And the present owner of the shawl is my mother. You, miss, are my birth mother," he said, looking at the maidservant. "As for who my birth father could be, I really have no idea. He might not even know himself. All I know is that he had no shame, leaving the girl in trouble like that."

Imi gave the magistrate a hard look, right in the eye.

With that, the maidservant, who was still unmarried, pulled

the shawl off the old woman's shoulders and held it tight.

"You're my son!" she shrieked.

The old woman stood quite still, however. She didn't reach for the shawl, just gazed at her little son as he stood between her and her husband.

Then the priest asked the magistrate, "Well now, your honour? Who does this child belong to? The woman who bore him, or the woman who raised him? What does the law have to say about it?"

But the law had nothing to say. The law was dumbstruck.

The magistrate gaped, first at the girl, then at the old woman, then at the little man, and said not a word.

Iron Imi went over to his birth mother and said, "Thank you, miss, for giving me life," and he gave her a bow. "I would like the shawl back, because it concerns me closely."

With that, he took the shawl from her. He turned and, taking his parents' hands, walked away with them. The magistrate, the maidservant, the priest and the villagers stood and watched them go. They were lost for words.

The little lad and his parents went home on foot. They were used to walking everywhere rather than riding on a cart like fine lords and ladies. It was Sunday, and Iron Imi never worked on a Sunday, as that was the day the Lord had declared should be a day of rest.

What he *did* do was gobble up three geese for dinner and wash them down with seven jugs of water and a mug of good, strong coffee. Then he sat out on the porch of the strong, stone house with his parents, like the lords and ladies, to count the clouds. And his parents started to tell him a story, because Iron Imi may have been strong and clever, but he loved a story as much as he loved plum jam. They told him a story about a child, a foundling child they had come across in the forest because the Lord God had put them all there for each other.

Dóra Gimesi

Margaret the Giant Killer

Once upon a time in Ireland, there was a small village by the sea. The people who lived there were quite ordinary. The women worked hard and the men said little. When a new ship came into the harbour bringing sailors from faraway lands, the villagers would narrow their eyes and look the foreigners up and down suspiciously. When Simon the Storyteller sailed into the village one evening in a tall ship, they did no differently.

Simon was a skinny young man with wild hair. Though he smiled freely and often, there was always a sadness of some sort in his eyes. While the crew loaded fresh supplies onto the ship, he went into the harbour pub to tell stories and sing for his supper.

"We don't reckon to pay for stories, round here," the barman muttered at him. "If you can't do any proper work, it'll be the high road for you."

Simon realised he would get no supper there that day. He sighed, tucked his guitar under his arm and headed back out to the jetty. He was hungry, and even though he was barely more than seventeen, just at that moment he felt incredibly old and weary.

He was nearly back at the ship when a voice suddenly spoke to him out of the dark.

"How many stories do you know?"

The voice came from behind him. Simon whirled around, startled. There stood a red-haired, freckled girl of fifteen

years old or so. Relieved, the storyteller gave a smile. "Lots."

"About heroes?"

"Some about heroes. I should tell you though, most stories are pretty much the same: the hero sets off on his journey, there's a bit of sword-fighting, some blood, more fighting, more blood, a kiss and a wedding. Pretty boring, really."

The girl pulled a face. "I know a story that isn't boring," she said.

Simon had been going from port to port as a wandering storyteller for many years. In the beginning, he had carefully noted down the names of the bays, the sandbanks and the rocky outcrops that featured in the stories the local people told him. But the more stories he heard, the more it became clear to him that it was only the places that changed. The stories were the same everywhere. He really didn't feel like going on with this conversation.

"What's it about?" he asked, more out of politeness than anything.

"I don't know yet. It hasn't started," replied the girl. "It's starting now. With you getting me on board your ship."

She wasn't asking him; she was telling him. Simon was so astonished, he forgot to protest. "And who's the hero in this story?"

The girl straightened up. "Well . . . me."

Just at that moment, the door of the pub burst open, and the barman stuck out his head. "Margaret!" he yelled at the top of his voice. "Where've you got to now? Damn you!"

The girl shuddered and moved into the shadow of the ship.

"You there! Waste of space!" shouted the barman to Simon. "Have you seen a crazy kitchenmaid out here?"

Simon looked at the girl, then at the barman and dumbly shook his head. When the pub door had banged shut again, the girl stepped out of the shadows.

"What's your name?" asked the storyteller. "Margaret who?"

"Margaret nothing. Just Margaret."

Simon shook his head. "That's no good. That's no name for a hero."

"Why not? What's a hero's name like then?" asked the girl.

"You know . . . heroic. A hero always needs to have an epithet. A name that tells you what he does. It's a kind of rule in stories. Richard the Lionheart, Brendan the Navigator, Robin Hood: Prince of Thieves . . ."

They sat on the jetty in silence for a while, musing and watching the water. From the pub came the sound of the barman swearing.

"Margaret, you ugly toad, you miserable, ham-fisted frog. Come out and show yourself this second, or I'll kick you out so hard your feet won't touch the ground!".

Margaret went red, but Simon hadn't heard a word. His mind was on something else.

"You know what?" he said. "We'll figure out what to call you on the way."

As they pulled out to sea, and the houses and the harbour dwindled into the distance, Margaret felt her heart swelling with happiness. She was free and she had never felt anything like it! She loved the wild wind, she loved the seagulls, even though they kept making a mess of the deck. She even loved being horribly seasick. And no matter how long she gazed at the blue, blue sea, she couldn't get enough of it.

They had been sailing for weeks when, one morning, some improbably dark clouds began to gather in the sky to the southwest. Clouds as black as ink.

Simon was standing in the bows with his telescope. He trained it on Margaret's face.

"It's about time you told me that story," he said to her.

"What story?"

"Your story. You said it wouldn't be boring."

"Well, it won't!" laughed Margaret. "Though not much has happened in it yet."

"All right, but what's going to happen now? Is there a knight coming in shining armour to carry you off as his wife? Or will it turn out that your father is a wealthy sultan from the East and he's going to announce a contest for your hand?"

Margaret shook her head. "I don't fancy either of those. I've got absolutely no desire to get married."

"But that's what girls in fairy tales usually do. They get married, then live happily ever after."

"But I don't want to be like the girls in fairy tales. I want to be a hero. I want to learn how to wield a sword, how to win at jousting tournaments and slay dragons."

"You're pretty ambitious for a girl."

"Don't believe me if you don't want to!"

As she stood there with a determined look in her eye, her red hair blowing about her face and the storm brewing behind her back, Margaret really did look as if she had stepped straight out of a story book. Simon caught himself wanting to kiss her.

"Well, that would definitely be a story I hadn't heard before," he said with an embarrassed grin. "But I do like the sound of it."

He might have gone on, but just then the ship suddenly rolled sideways, and a huge wave crashed onto the deck.

"The storm's here!" roared the helmsman.

He was wrong though. Behind the ship, an enormous monster, more like a snake or a dragon than anything else, was rising out of the sea, its jaws gaping.

"There's flesh of Ireland on your ship. I could smell it for miles!" it boomed. "There's flesh of Ireland on your ship! Let me have it, if you value your lives!"

"Bring up the beef," said Simon, giving the order before panic could break out among the crew.

The sailors packed the dried beef they had bought in the Irish port into a big chest and threw it into the sea.

The monster gobbled it up, and disappeared, satisfied, into the deep.

"You're pretty brave for a storyteller," commented Margaret.

"It's not a question of being brave," said the boy, shrugging his shoulders. "Every fairy tale has a monster in it. If we let it have what it wants, it won't bother anyone."

Simon was wrong though. Hardly an hour and a half had gone by before the sea monster once again rose out of the water. Its jaws were stretched wide enough to swallow the ship whole.

"There's flesh of Ireland on your ship. I could smell it for miles! There's flesh of Ireland on your ship! Let me have it, if you value your lives!" it boomed.

"Your nose is deceiving you, you cur! You've had all the beef there is already!" yelled Simon. "We brought nothing else from Ireland."

The sea monster was undeterred. "You lie! You did bring something else! You brought tender, white flesh of Ireland!"

Simon tried to protest but a mighty wave came and knocked him down. He was thrown against the rail of the ship like a rag doll.

"I will smash your ship into smithereens. I will drown every one of your crew! Give me Irish flesh, Simon! If there's no beef, give me human flesh!" growled the monster.

Simon lay in the bows of the ship, only half alive. When he finally managed to open his eyes, he saw Margaret and the sea serpent glaring at each other.

"Is it me you want, monster?"

The sea monster nodded eagerly.

"In your dreams!" grunted Simon, scrambling to his feet with great difficulty. Margaret rushed over to help him up.

"I wheedled my way on board your ship. This is all my fault," she said hurriedly. "If you don't give me up to the monster, you'll all be lost."

"No, I won't let you go," said the storyteller.

It was no use, however. Margaret had already decided what she was going to do, and nothing was going to sway her.

"I left home to be a hero. This is my first adventure. If I survive it, fine, but if I don't, please tell my story in every port. Tell them about Margaret the Selfless, who was not scared of the sea monster. If that's too short, you can dress it up a bit."

"But that's a stupid name! And, anyway, the hero can't die in the middle of the story!" Simon shouted after her.

Margaret couldn't hear him, however. She had jumped into one of the lifeboats and was signalling to the helmsman to lower it into the water. The next moment, a towering wave came and snatched up the little boat.

"Come on, monster, catch me if you can!" shouted Margaret. She saw the monster throwing itself after the boat, but then she lost her balance, fell over and banged her head.

When she came to, Margaret found herself in a little hut on an unfamiliar, rocky shore. Her head was aching terribly, she was hungry and cold, but at least she was alive.

"Finally!" said a hoarse voice. It didn't sound very friendly.

A little, wrinkled old woman was leaning over her. There were long, grey hairs curling out of the woman's nose.

Margaret said the first thing that came into her head. "Are you a witch?"

The old woman looked down her nose at Margaret indignantly. "Mind your manners, young lady!"

"I'm sorry. I didn't mean . . . I just wanted to thank you for saving my life."

"Well, there's a price to pay for it," grinned the witch. "Now you have to tell me your heart's desire."

Without a moment's hesitation, Margaret told her. "I want to be a hero," she said.

The witch nodded.

"You're not surprised?" asked Margaret. "You're not going to tell me that's a strange thing for a girl to want?"

"I don't think there's anything strange about it at all. If you're willing to put the work in, you'll find you can learn a thing or two here."

Margaret was an excellent student. Before a year had gone by, she had learned how to climb trees, how to swim across fast-flowing rivers and how to wield a sword. She learned which plants were poisonous and which had healing properties. She could recognise the minerals hidden away in caves and she learned to read the stars in the night sky. The witch (or fairy – Margaret was still unsure about this long afterwards) was a strict and painstaking teacher. And it was impossible to lie to her.

"What are you afraid of?" the witch asked once, when they were sitting by the fire.

"I'm not afraid of anything," Margaret shot back.

"Rubbish!" growled the witch. "Everyone's afraid of something. Why did you leave your village?"

"I wanted to see the world."

"And?"

"So I could be a hero."

"And?"

"So that storytellers would tell my story."

The old woman's eyes narrowed to a slit. "Poppycock!" she said at last. "Why did you really leave?"

Margaret stared into the fire. In the crackling and spitting of the logs she heard familiar voices crowing, sniggering and yelling, and in the leaping flames she saw people she knew making horrible faces at her.

Margaret, fetch those fish!
Quick, bring in the water!
Why can't you embroider,
Like a good, well-mannered daughter?

Get to work. Stop dreaming
Of ships and far-flung lands,
Kill that chicken, go on!
The knife is in your hands!

Look at her among the hens,
Mama, she's trying to joust!
Whatever are you doing, girl?
Sit up straight, don't slouch!

You'll never get a husband.
You'll be a sad old maid.
Butterfingers, freckle-face,
You'll never make the grade!

Margaret pressed her lips together.

"I know what you're hearing now," said the old woman.

"You do?"

"That's the voice of the giant. He's been rampaging through this land for centuries. The day is coming when you will have to fight him face to face."

Margaret leapt to her feet. This was the task she had been longing for all her life. "Where is he? Show me the giant and I'll fight him. I'll slice him into shreds!"

The old woman smiled. "Patience, my child. When the time is right."

One morning, when the first snowdrops were poking up out of the frozen ground, a traveller came along the shore and knocked on the door of the hut. He was tall and skinny, his tangled hair hung in his eyes, and his chin was covered in a beard of many days' growth. Despite this, Margaret recognised him the moment she laid her eyes on him. It was Simon, the storyteller. There was no time to think or feel shy, she just threw her arms around his neck,

and gave him a long, long hug.

Over the next few days, they went on long walks together, and not for a moment did they run out of things to say to each other. Simon told Margaret how he had wandered for years, seeking her on uninhabited islands, in faraway lands and in the stories told by superstitious old sailors. Margaret told Simon everything she had learned from the old woman.

On the evening of the third day, all three of them were sitting by the fire.

"I'm going to fight a terrible, man-eating giant," Margaret announced proudly.

This time, she was surprised to find that the witch did not mutter, "Aye, when you're ready." Instead, she turned to Margaret and gave her a solemn look. "You still want to fight him?"

"More than anything," replied Margaret.

"Then you can set off first thing tomorrow morning," said the old woman.

Margaret started making preparations immediately. She had never been so happy in all her life. She was just polishing her sword, when Simon came over and crouched down on a tree stump next to her. There was clearly something he wanted to say, but he was having trouble finding the words.

"Don't do it! Don't go and fight the giant," he finally blurted out. "Giants are horribly strong. The greatest heroes, the bravest knights go off to fight them, and sometimes one will succeed, but most of them never come back."

Margaret looked at him indignantly. "Well, I'm certainly coming back," she said. "If you're so afraid of the giant, just be glad you don't need to fight him." With that, she picked up her sword and went into the hut.

The night was clear and cold. Simon tried to sleep, but the rustling from the nearby wood, the quickening spring breezes, the ticking of the woodworm in the trees all seemed

to be whispering familiar words in his ear. The sniggers of
his old schoolmates, orders shouted at fencing lessons, the
drumming of horses' hooves in the dust of the tilt yard all
came together to form an ugly little ditty:

> *Grab his sword, punch his nose!*
> *Climb on his back, cut his throat!*
> *Stop that snivelling, stop that bawling!*
> *That's right, run away! Always stalling!*
> *Simon the scaredy-cat, weakling, wimp!*
> *Lily-livered, coward, such a shrimp!*

Simon sat up on his bed of hay, but even while he was
awake the voices surrounded him. Dawn had barely broken
when he gathered up his things and crept out of the hut.

"I wouldn't go where you're going without a sword,"
came a hoarse voice from behind him. The old woman was
standing in the doorway, leaning on the lintel, her face lit
only when the embers in her pipe glowed red.

"I left Margaret in the lurch once before. I won't do it
again," said Simon.

The witch looked him up and down. Her eyes narrowed.
"Why did you become a travelling storyteller? Most boys
like you are training to be knights."

"I like good stories."

"And?"

"I wasn't such a great swordsman."

"And?"

Simon felt as if the woman could see right through him.
"Everyone expected that one day I would be a hero. But I'm
not the hero type."

The witch smiled and held out an old sword to him. "All
right, Simon. Now you can go and fight the giant."

Half an hour later, Margaret came out of the hut. Her red
hair was pinned up and a shiny sword hung from her waist.

"It suits you," laughed the old woman. "But hurry, that lad is already on his way. He thinks he can protect you from the giant, poor thing!"

Margaret asked no questions. She just ran. She ran through the woods, up the hill and straight towards the rocky heights where the giants lived.

Milk-white fog was drifting through the land of the giants, and it was miserably cold and damp. Simon could hear the creature's voice all the time now. Its laughter was there, whistling among the treetops. Its scornful words were pounding in his ears. On all sides, the rocks looked like faces he knew; mocking, hateful faces.

Suddenly, something snapped behind him. He turned and pointed his sword at it. To his great relief, the shape emerging from the fog was Margaret.

"I owe you an apology," she said. "I didn't mean to suggest you were a coward."

"Apology accepted," said Simon, nodding. "And I didn't mean to question your heroism."

There was more he wanted to say, but just then a terrifying wind swept through the landscape, making everything shake. The fog cleared for a moment, then rolled into the space between them, even thicker and colder than before. They couldn't see each other, and though they called out, the fog was like cotton wool and swallowed up their voices. They couldn't hear anything except the creaking of the hollow trees and what sounded like the rush of a great bird's wings.

Margaret drew her sword. "Come on then, giant!" she shouted into the fog. "Show yourself, come out and fight a duel with me!"

The giant gave a laugh. It was a terrifying laugh, mocking, scathing and hateful. Margaret heard in it the voices of the children and the men and women of her village.

"Look at her! Look at that crazy little knock-kneed girl!
Look at those freckles! Look at her two left feet!"

Margaret thrust her sword towards the sound. She lunged
again and again. She couldn't see her enemy for the fog, so
she closed her eyes and let the voices guide her. The giant
winced, as if he had been wounded.

"Not bad, for a girl. But if you think you can be a hero,
you are very much mistaken. You're just a little girl with
a big sword, whom no one wanted. No one loves you,
little Margaret."

"That's not true!" shouted Margaret, slicing at empty fog.

"Give up, little girl, give yourself up, and I will give you
what you have never had. Put down that ugly sword. It's not
for the likes of you. Put down the sword and, in an instant,
all the goodness, all the charm, all the beauty in the world
will be yours and everyone will love you, you'll see. Even that
scrawny lad you brought with you. You'll have a new story,
and a new name: you'll be Margaret the Beautiful."

The giant's words seemed to be coming from every leaf,
every breeze and every gaping cave. Margaret could hear the
giant's whispering even in the beating of her own heart.
Bewitched, she gazed into the fog. Slowly, she bent over, and
laid the sword down at her feet.

At that moment, she heard a voice from behind, a voice
she knew well.

"That's a pretty boring name, if you ask me."

It was Simon, standing on a flat stone, sword in hand.
The giant roared and lunged towards him. A furious,
bleeding face emerged from the fog, huge yellow eyes
blinking and searching for their prey.

"What did you say, you lily-livered wimp? I'll grind your
bones . . ."

"Yes, yes . . . to make your bread. You've snapped greater
heroes than me in half before now. But before you do that,
let me tell you a little story."

The giant had already raised his fist but was so astonished at this that his great hand stopped in mid-air.

Simon began.

"There was once a boy who was not born to be a hero. He was scrawny and a bit of a dreamer. Swords were too heavy for him, and he would faint at the sight of blood. He was, let's admit it, not very brave. In fact, he was a coward. He was so terrified of having to be a hero, that he would rather spend his whole life telling other people's stories."

"You're a coward, a coward," echoed the giant, but Simon kept straight on.

"That's what I'm telling you. But there's more. This boy was such a coward that when he fell in love with a girl, he didn't dare tell her. He was such a coward that he would rather go off and fight a giant and be snapped in two, have his bones ground up and baked into bread . . ."

"I'll eat you up!" roared the giant. His breath nearly

knocked Simon over backwards.

"And do you know what that girl was called? The one the cowardly boy fell in love with? Her name was Margaret the Giant Killer."

At that moment, Margaret's sword dealt a great blow to the giant's neck. Now able to see to her enemy, she had taken careful aim. The shrieks of the dying giant echoed around the rocks, startling a flock of crows out of a bush.

Then there was silence. Margaret and Simon sat down on the flat stone and watched as the fog slowly drifted away and the sun came out from behind the rocks.

"What now?" asked Simon. "How does the story go on?"

Margaret burst out laughing. "How should I know? You're the storyteller."

"All right then. But you won't mind if I put in a wedding?"

"It's not terribly original, but if you insist . . ." said Margaret, shrugging her shoulders.

From that day forward, Simon the Storyteller and Margaret the Giant Killer travelled the world together. Margaret went around slaying monsters and dragons. Jousting tournaments were named after her and little girls tried their best to be like her. For his part, Simon told fantastically exciting stories about the adventures they shared. These stories were passed from mouth to mouth and from generation to generation.

There are people telling them even to this day.

Edit Szűcs

Koni's Antlers

The first thing the little fawn laid eyes on was the sunlight filtering down through the needles of a pine tree. While his mother licked him clean, he marvelled at the orange sky and listened to the twittering of the birds.

"My sweet little Koni," said his mother. "I'm so glad you're here!"

Koni was only a few weeks old when his mother decided it was time for him to get to know some other fawns. One day, when the sun was setting, she took him out into the meadow. An old friend of hers was waiting there with her own fawn. Koni's mother introduced her son to Mara and her young fawn, who, skipped up to Koni, laughing merrily, and introduced himself as Ronan.

"Still getting the hang of her legs, is she? She'll make a lovely doe, though!" said Mara.

For some reason, this compliment made Koni feel bad.

"I don't want anyone calling me a doe," he muttered, and to show how nimble he was, he leapt to his feet. But his legs got tangled up with each other, and he ended up doing a somersault. He heard Ronan snigger and felt hurt. Koni slunk a little further off.

Ronan galloped up to him and butted him apologetically. Koni soon forgot his embarrassment, and before long they were firm friends.

From then on, Koni and Ronan met up nearly every day. Koni got to know other deer and some of the other animals too. He really liked the fox because he knew lots of good jokes. He liked the pine marten because he played

hide-and-seek with him. His most memorable meeting, however, was with his father.

Koni and his mother were in the meadow, and Koni was just in the middle of a game with Ronan and the other bucks, when his mother called him over. She wasn't alone. Beside her was a stag, taller than any Koni had ever seen. His head was crowned with a beautiful pair of branching antlers, and he held himself so proudly that the little fawn couldn't help feeling a little frightened of him. When the stag bent down to him and smiled, however, Koni no longer felt afraid.

As he trotted back to his friends, he heard his father say to his mother, "What a beautiful daughter we have!"

Koni suddenly didn't feel like playing any more.

That first lovely summer did not last for ever. The days got colder and colder and shorter and shorter, and Koni noticed that his mother was becoming more and more nervous. They saw less and less of Ronan and his mother, instead spending most of their time searching for food, as the vegetation slowly died back.

"We'll have to be careful where we go now," Koni's mother warned him. "There are fewer and fewer leaves on the trees to hide us from the hunters."

Koni heard the fear in his mother's voice when she talked about the hunters, but he didn't understand it. He kept to the new rules, though, and burrowed into the fallen leaves as if he knew exactly what kind of danger was out there watching them.

One day in late autumn, when there was such a cold wind in the mornings that Koni had practically no feeling in his hooves, he and his mother set off to join the herd. They would huddle together until the warm days returned. Koni was delighted. He could hardly wait to see Ronan again, and maybe also his father.

He was to be disappointed however. All the deer were

anxious, and the puzzled fawns stayed close to their parents. Koni could hear bangs in the distance, and he too didn't dare stray far from his mother.

Suddenly, Ronan burst out of the bushes at the edge of the woods. He looked terrified. His mother was no longer with him.

They passed a miserable winter. Koni hadn't realised that their food would not last for ever, that there would come a time when they would have to chew tree bark. Ronan was less talkative than before. He stayed with Koni and his mother for a while, then, as the end of winter approached and the herd split up, he too disappeared.

By the spring, much had changed. Koni had grown taller and had lost his white spots. The days grew longer, and the snow melted. The woods became more peaceful, and though several of their dearest friends had vanished during the winter, never to be seen again, hope returned to the hearts of the animals.

When Koni first went to the meadow to meet up with the other young deer, he was faced with something he had always been afraid would happen. While the top of his head was unchanged, the other bucks had started to grow antlers. Among the bucks, Koni spotted his father. He ran over, hoping for some advice. "Dad, when will my antlers grow?" he asked.

His father looked surprised. "Well, if you're anything like me, they'll start growing pretty soon. Your mother will be able to tell you," he replied uncertainly.

Buoyed by this news, Koni ran back to the others. Later, though, he noticed his parents were arguing about something. Koni felt strange. He wanted to play with the other bucks like he used to, but they kept sending him away, saying he couldn't fight with them without antlers. Koni walked slowly back to his mother, dragging his feet.

"Mum? When will my antlers grow so I can play with the other bucks?"

"Koni! It's time to stop this nonsense! You know very well that you will never have antlers. You can't play with the bucks any more. It's time you got to know the other hinds."

The other hinds.

"What are you talking about, Mum?"

"You've got to stop this fantasising, Koni. You'll be a grown-up soon!"

His mother sighed and walked off, leaving Koni alone.

Koni was so confused, he burst into tears. He realised too that he was no longer happy having a hind's name. But he didn't know what to do about it. He missed Ronan and was more afraid each day that he would never see his friend again. Koni was inconsolable.

That was the day Koni first went off without his mother. He wanted to be away from the other deer for a while, so he went to look for his animal friends. At twilight, Koni was talking to the fox, when a stranger appeared. But no, this buck was no stranger . . . it was Ronan! He looked so different. He had grown a crown of antlers. Koni tried to keep down the envy that was rising inside him. They greeted each other by touching foreheads, then told each other what had happened to them since the snow had melted. Koni told him his troubles: that he had no antlers, that the others wouldn't accept him as a buck and that he didn't like his old name any longer either.

Ronan had an answer to the last of these complaints right away. "What do you think of *Konor*?"

"Konor," murmured his friend. "It's perfect!"

From that moment on, Konor, proudly bearing his new name, spent more time with his father and Ronan. His mother wasn't willing to call him by his new name, his real name. Konor didn't want to argue, so, even though it made him sad, he avoided spending time with her.

He was still bothered by his lack of antlers though. He could see that, apart from Ronan, none of the other took

him seriously. When he paraded past the hinds, his head held high, more often than not he would hear sniggering.

These were difficult times for Konor, but his woodland friends did their best to cheer him up. Ronan showed him how to behave like a buck and was even willing to fight with him, despite the fact that, with no antlers to get in the way, Ronan was able to headbutt his friend and knock him onto his backside over and over.

The woodland animals tried to make Konor some antlers. The fox mixed up some mud, which the squirrel and the pine marten spread on his head. Then two birds each brought a branch and stuck them into the mud. Another time, they wove twine from long weeds and used it to tie large pinecones onto Konor's head. None of these solutions lasted very long, but each unsuccessful attempt made Konor laugh, and inside he was grateful to his friends for their help. It gave him the chance to feel like a proud buck for a while. The other animals clapped and encouraged him, so that, briefly, he was able to feel that all was well.

One afternoon in late summer, a swallow joined the crowd of animals watching as Konor and Ronan charged at each other, Konor wearing antlers made of wood this time. The two branches flew in opposite directions, and the two bucks, dizzy from the impact, tried to gather themselves together.

"Well, that's the end of those antlers," sighed the fox.

"What is it you're trying so hard to do?" asked the swallow, curious.

"They're trying to make me a pair of antlers," explained Konor, still flailing around on the ground.

"And why don't they just get hold of a pair of real antlers?"

"You mean ones that other deer have shed? We've tried that too," replied the fox. "Old antlers fall off just as quickly as branches."

"No! I mean real ones! *Real*, real ones!" said the swallow, chirping merrily.

Konor looked up. "How do we do that?" he asked in astonishment.

"You need to find the Spring Fairy! He brings all the changes that there are in the world. I'm sure he could help you."

"And where can we find him? Where do we need to go?" asked Konor. He couldn't believe the answer was so simple.

"There's no use going anywhere now. You can only find the Spring Fairy in the spring, and you can't hurry that," said the swallow.

"And he's bound to want something in return," said the fox. "You don't get anything for free, these days. Swallow, will this fairy grant anyone's wish?"

"I've heard that only those who are worthy get their wishes granted."

Worthy? thought Konor. *It won't be so easy after all, then.*

"What would Konor have to do to prove himself worthy?" asked Ronan.

"Well . . ." the swallow was starting, but Konor cut in.

"Why should I have to prove myself worthy?" he asked crossly. "The other bucks haven't done anything special to earn their antlers! Why should I have to?"

The others went quiet. No one knew what to say to that. Eventually, Ronan went over to his friend, and butted him gently in the side. "I'm sorry. You're right, it really isn't fair."

Konor heaved a great sigh. "But look on the bright side, Konor. You'll get your antlers!"

They smiled at each other.

"If I may say something . . ." said the swallow softly. "I don't know what the Spring Fairy might be expecting, but I think you should try to perform a heroic deed of some kind. That ought to do it. Good luck!"

After the swallow's visit, Konor did a lot of walking in the woods, trying to think who he could help. No one was in need of heroic deeds just then. Deep in his heart, he was still angry at how unfair it was that he had to prove

himself worthy of something the other bucks just got as
a matter of course. Some days, he felt that when he found
the fairy, he would rather give him a telling-off for putting
up with such a wicked world.

The other deer had begun to behave strangely too. The
bucks' playful butting turned into real battles for territory
and hinds. Konor couldn't see the point of these fights.
The only thing he would be willing to fight for was a set of
antlers. Ronan too was pulled into these fights, which made
Konor very unhappy. He didn't like seeing his friend covered
in scratches, and he was also upset by the thought that
Ronan might decide to spend his life with someone else.
Konor just wanted everything to get back to normal.

One afternoon, when he was walking up and down the
tracks in the woods, he bumped into Ronan. His friend's
coat looked a little matted, but Konor was glad to see him.
His delight lasted until he spotted another buck behind
Ronan. Konor knew this other buck. They had played
together as fawns, but Konor had never liked him because
he was rough.

Both bucks looked angry. Konor moved towards Ronan,
but the other buck leapt between them. That was when
Konor realised that this idiot wanted to fight for him.

For him and not *with* him.

The buck turned towards Konor. "You either come with
me of your own accord, Koni, or Ronan and I will fight
for you."

Konor had had enough. When the buck turned towards
Ronan ready to attack him, Konor charged with all his
strength and butted him in the side. *I can get on just fine
without antlers,* he thought. The buck went flying. Shocked
and sore, he ran off.

"What was he thinking?" said Konor, indignantly. "Are
you hurt?" he asked his friend, who had come to nestle up
against him.

Ronan promised that he would stay with Konor and that
they would defend each other if need be. They slept under
the starry sky, huddled close together against the cold.

On their autumn walks, Konor, his father and Ronan
helped the woodland creatures prepare for winter. They
helped the pine marten find a winter den and the fox to
gather fallen leaves for a winter blanket. Konor got to know
every corner of the woods.

When the last few leaves began to drift down through the
grey woodland, Konor sensed that the hunters would soon
be with them.

He didn't have to wait long.

One morning, at dawn, they woke to the cries of deer.
As they leaped out of their hiding places, Konor's father
appeared by their side to hurry them along. They began to
run from the rumble of the guns. More and more animals
jumped out and ran off in fright. In the confusion, Ronan
disappeared from sight.

Konor and his father were running alongside a clearing
when Konor heard something. "Father, wait! Isn't that the
sound of fawns crying?"

They froze. His father pricked up his ears.

"You're right. They're over there," shouted his father and
flung himself into the bushes that fringed the meadow,
Konor close on his tail.

A horrible sight met their eyes. Two young fawns stood
wailing pitifully by the body of their mother, so upset they
didn't dare leave her side.

Without a moment's hesitation, Konor and his father
dashed towards them. Konor nudged the fawns to get to them
to move away, while his father covered the three of them.
At that moment, Konor saw something glinting between the
trees. They began to run in the other direction, towards the
safety of the woods, when they heard another bang.

It's never been so loud, thought Konor. *Why is it so loud?*

They leapt through the bushes and kept on running. Then suddenly there were only three of them. His father was no longer with them.

At long last, they reached the other deer, who were huddled together, terrified. The two little fawns were trembling, and Konor, too, could go no further. Luckily, Ronan was there with the herd. He was trying to keep them in order, but when he saw Konor, he ran over and nestled up to him.

Konor backed away. His mother was there, and everyone he knew. He couldn't look them in the eye. "Look after the fawns, please! Find them a home," he whispered, pushing them towards Ronan.

Then he turned round and started running.

Konor blamed himself for what had happened to his father, whom he knew would never return. He was so ashamed, he hid himself away. He took paths only his father had known. For a long time, he didn't want to eat, so day by day he became weaker. He wouldn't have survived the winter if his old woodland friends hadn't found him and returned the help he had given them. The fox brought Konor food and snuggled up to him when the cold blizzards came. The pine marten sat quietly with him when he wanted some company. It wasn't easy, but they made it through to the day the first snowdrop opened.

It's time to go back, thought Konor, early one March morning. He was still sad and sorry for what had happened to his father, but he felt ready.

He was making his way home and the woods were beginning to look familiar, when he caught sight of a man. No, not a man . . . A strange, tousled figure the size of a small child with the legs of a goat. It seemed to be making flowers grow beside the roots of a tree.

Konor gazed in wonder. *Was it the Spring Fairy?* He had forgotten all about his plan to ask for a pair of real antlers.

And now he didn't feel prepared. *I haven't performed any heroic deeds. What shall I do?*

He approached the scruffy creature, who turned towards him and greeted him with a smile. The young buck started to explain how and why he had ended up here in this part of the wood.

The fairy listened carefully. "And you thought I would expect a heroic deed in exchange for helping you? Don't be silly! Everyone deserves to live in a way that is true to themselves. And anyway, you're already a hero. Don't think I haven't heard of you! Every animal in these woods knows your name, Konor. It has meant a great deal to them, having you around. Not to mention the two little fawns . . ."

When the fairy saw that the buck had started to cry, he reached over and rubbed his neck. "I'm just sorry I couldn't be here earlier," he said. Then his face fell. "I hope you won't be disappointed, but I'm afraid I can't give you antlers. I only have power over the plants of the woods. The most I can do is put two fine-looking branches on your head, which will always be with you. What do you say?"

Konor, of course, said yes.

At this, the fairy called together the buck's woodland friends, who set about searching for the two most beautiful branches in the wood. The fairy placed these between Konor's ears and kissed him on the top of his head. At that moment, the two branches became part of his body.

"Will you do something for me now? Will you continue to take good care of the creatures living in these woods?" asked the fairy. "I hope you will be happier in the future than you have been so far," he said, and bid them goodbye.

Konor thanked his friends for everything they had done, then he resumed his journey home. He could hardly wait to get there.

The first deer he saw were the two little fawns that he and Ronan had rescued. One of them was doing a somersault

in the grass as it played
with Ronan.

When Konor saw Ronan,
his heart began to beat faster.
The herd looked up at the
approach of the stranger, and
for a moment not even Ronan
recognised him.

"Konor!" he cried out and
ran over to him, delighted.

As they met, their antlers
got tangled up. They laughed
as they tried to disentangle
them. Konor had never felt
so happy.

Lots of things changed in
the woods after that day.
Though he still got them
caught in low-hanging
branches, Konor slowly got
used to his new antlers. They
blossomed in springtime, and
if they got broken off, they
always sprouted again.
Cheerful and confident, Konor
finally felt comfortable in his
own skin.

The other deer were glad to
have him back with them.
From that time on, they all
thought of him as a buck, and
his beautiful antlers were the
subject of much admiration.
Even Konor's mother came to
find him one day to make

peace with him. She called him "my son" at last. Konor forgave her just as he had forgiven the other deer, but he preferred to spend his days with his old friends and his new family.

Konor took the two little fawns that Ronan had adopted under his wing too. He and Ronan brought them up together. They still liked to wander along the woodland trails and were often joined on their evening walks by their friends. The pine marten would stretch out on their backs. The fox would trot along beside the two young fawns, and the birds would perch in Konor's antlers. Konor loved these walks. He often thought with gratitude of the Spring Fairy, and, true to his promise, he took care of the woodland creatures all the days of his life.

Edit Pengő

The Kidnapped Princess

Once upon a time, there lived a prince who was very sad. His name was Benedek. He had blue eyes and golden-blond hair and was so short that even his three younger sisters were taller than he was. Benedek was sad because, of all his brothers and sisters, he was the only one his parents were not proud of. His sisters had all found a husband and had children. They managed merry, interesting royal households which were a pleasure to visit. His older brothers had become heroic knights and had commanded their father's troops in battle.

The king and queen worried about when Benedek would finally find his place in the world. They sent him to the best fencing masters in the country, but their expertise did not rub off on him. They presented him with an excellent steed, but he didn't dare mount it – to his parents' shame, he could only handle ponies. The only thing he showed any talent for was archery, but he didn't have enough of that to add a fox fur or a pair of antlers to the collection of hunting trophies in the palace trophy room.

Benedek was glum, his parents were glum, the whole kingdom was glum.

One morning, Benedek came upon an intriguing notice in the small ads section of the newspaper that had been set out on the breakfast table beside his scrambled eggs and ham:

Ferrum seeks a dragon-slaying hero!
A wicked, fire-breathing monster has carried off the princess.
The reward for her rescue: the princess's hand in marriage!
Knightly title and steed not required.
Apply at the palace gates.

Password: I'll Get Her Back!

Ferrum was the neighbouring kingdom and famous for its sword making. The blades made there were magnificent and could cut through anything. This was lucky for the people of Ferrum, because if it weren't for that, no one would have talked to their miserly king.

All day, Benedek wondered about whether he should go to Ferrum to free the princess. He, a dragon-slayer? He, a husband? He couldn't even hold his sword straight! And whenever he got on a horse he ended up on the ground – just that day he had landed in the only puddle for miles around . . . twice! He would end up a laughing stock, in his parents' eyes and in the eyes of the whole world.

But what if he were successful? If only he could see pride in his parents' eyes when they looked at him. He wouldn't have to run the monster through with his sword. He could shoot it down with his bow, wound it in the eye, and while the dragon was rolling about in pain, he could free the girl. He would bring even greater glory to the empire than his brothers had done!

At first light, Benedek saddled up his pony and, disguising himself as a servant so the peasants wouldn't see how their prince was travelling, he set off on the road that led to Ferrum. He left a message for his parents saying that he would only return when he had become worthy of them.

He was warmly received at the palace in Ferrum. The gatekeeper led him to the antechamber right away and informed the king of his arrival.

"His Majesty is very busy, but hopefully he will soon make time to give you your instructions."

The gatekeeper's hopes, however, were not fulfilled. Benedek waited all day to be summoned. It was dinnertime before his name was called. The king was standing by the door, his head bowed. When he heard Benedek's footsteps, he straightened up, and with a show of determination, turned towards the newcomer. He was disappointed to see a short boy dressed as a servant, but rather than sending him away, he acquainted the boy briefly with the task ahead of him.

"The monster came here just as my daughter was getting married and decided to ruin the wedding. It crushed the dome of the church, and in plain sight of the world's finest knights, snatched Gabriella from her bridegroom's side. Those fine knights all chased after it, only to return thoroughly singed and scorched. I was forced to send the humiliated bridegroom after them. The dragon's cave is on Mount Vertigo. Just follow the trail of charred trees to find the way. If you are successful, my daughter's hand . . ." Here, the king, struggling with his emotions, cleared his throat. ". . . is yours. Hurry! You can imagine the harm this is doing to our business! We have never sold so few swords. Who wants to buy a sword from a king who can't get his own daughter back?"

As soon as Benedek had finished talking to the king, he embarked on the rescue mission. He soon found the road to the dragon's cave. Everything was just as the king had said. Blackened tree trunks and armour thrown aside by the retreating knights showed him which way to go.

The entrance to the cave loomed darkly on the top of a rocky peak. It would have been difficult to approach in daylight, let alone at night, so Benedek chose instead to take shelter in the hollow of a tree. He was exhausted and fell asleep instantly.

He woke to a horrible howling sound. The dragon, a huge

beast covered in green scales, was crowing triumphantly in
the entrance to the cave. Just then, a tall knight rolled off
the rock which he had been trying to climb in full armour.
Reaching the ground, the knight began to proclaim his
burning love for Gabriella, at which the dragon started
roaring all over again. The knight had no choice but to
gallop off at breakneck speed.

Benedek went cold with fear. Was this the monster he had
to fight? It was huge and bristling with claws and tusks!
His arrows would turn back at the mere sight of it!

"If he comes back again, I'll give him a talking to myself,"
said a girl's voice from close by. "He's tried to rescue me
more times than the number of hours we were engaged!"

Gabriella appeared by the dragon's side. She was wearing
boy's clothes and had cut her hair short, but it was
definitely her, the kidnapped princess. She was doing a good
job of concealing her terror of the monster towering over
her. It almost looked as if the two of them were having

a friendly chat. Surely not!

Benedek spent the day observing his opponent. After chasing away the knight, the dragon flew down to a garden to pick vegetables. The creature's kidnapped victim remained in the cave. Instead of trying to escape, she hung the washing out to dry, slaving for her captor. At noon, they made lunch from the vegetables the dragon had collected – Benedek watched their every move lest Gabriella end up in the soup. Then in the afternoon they flew off to some nearby fields.

Evening was coming by the time Gabriella returned. She got back a few hours after the dragon, climbing up to the cave by a hidden path. With an empty, rumbling stomach, Benedek listened to the sounds that carried down from the top of the mountain: the clattering of plates, conversation and laughter.

At nightfall, Benedek crept out of his hiding place and, following the path he had seen the princess use, he made his way up to the rocky peak. He was here to rescue Gabriella! He couldn't leave her in the dragon's claws to . . . live happily ever after?!

He stole into the cave. Out of the darkness, a voice addressed him.

"I was wondering when you were going to come out of that tree." Gabriella was smiling at him, hands on hips.

"I didn't know . . ." Benedek began, in a rush of embarrassment. Then, putting on a show of determination, he went on, "I'm here to rescue you!"

"Of course you are! Come on, there's a little dinner left. Baldur's gone to bed, so try to keep the noise down. He's a terribly bad sleeper." Seeing Benedek's alarm, she added, "He won't bite your head off, even if you do wake him up. Relax!"

In the morning, Baldur greeted Benedek cheerily. In a deep, purring voice, he remarked that it was all the same to

him how many little men set up camp in his cave; Benedek should feel free to stay. He should just be careful not to get trampled to death.

This was how Benedek was welcomed to his new home.

"What do you like doing?" Gabriella asked Benedek.

"I don't really know," he replied, after some thought.

"Well, what kind of things do you usually do?"

"Sword-fighting, riding . . ."

"All right, let's try again. Do you fancy painting my room?"

"Painting your room? I've never . . . I'd make a mess of it. I'm no good at girls' stuff."

"Painting's not girls' stuff! Are you going to help, or do I have to beg you?"

They spent all day painting Gabriella's chamber in the cave. First, they selected the colours, then they discussed what images to paint and where: a deer by Gabriella's bed, a family of dragons on the ceiling and green branches around the entrance. Benedek enjoyed the work, and he didn't make a mess of it. Even Baldur did a good job, though he found the brush difficult to hold between his claws. After a while, he went out to the kitchen, preferring to bake a carrot cake with his armour-melting fire.

At bedtime, Benedek realised he had forgotten to ask Gabriella about the kidnapping.

The next day, he made sure to ask. Gabriella told him that ever since she had come of age, her father had been trying to marry her off. After the umpteenth failed engagement, she had realised that she had no problem with any of the young knights and ladies. It was just that she wasn't interested in romance. She had liked many of the suitors her father had lined up for her and would gladly have been their friend. But marrying them? She just didn't fancy it. Her father had told her if she just waited, the right person would come along. He had herded guests into the palace one after the other. Then, running out of patience, he announced a jousting tournament and told his daughter she would marry the champion, no ifs or buts.

Hearing this, Gabriella had decided to write to her mother, Gréta. Not since the princess was small had Gréta been involved in Gabriella's upbringing. She had been unhappy at Ferrum palace and had run away, leaving her daughter behind. Later, Gabriella had tracked her down and they had written to each other and even met from time to time. They had grown apart, but Gabriella hoped that she could count on her mother if she were ever in real trouble. And she was right: Gréta had sent Baldur to fetch her away. She would have liked her daughter to go and live with her in the Empire of the Dragons, but Gabriella preferred to stay with Baldur.

Benedek grew to love living with Gabriella and Baldur. They spent their days doing jobs around the cave, working their way through Baldur's library and relaxing. The princess and the dragon found new hobbies for Benedek: drawing and sewing. Benedek taught Gabriella archery. And the two young people helped Baldur realise a dream he had nursed for three hundred years. He wanted to start up a cake-baking business. They made long journeys, flying to faraway countries to sell the cakes he made.

Benedek put his skill at sewing to use making soft toys. He sewed toys for children, adults and for his new friends, of course. Even Baldur got a cushion in the shape of a giant crocodile.

One day, when Benedek was looking for fresh sewing materials, he came across Gabriella's old dress. It was all sequins and ruffles, not comfortable or practical at all. It didn't even have pockets, so it was no wonder that Gabriella had consigned it to the back of the wardrobe. Benedek decided he would put it to rights. Keeping the feminine cut, he removed the surplus flounces, and added material where it was needed. He did a lovely job on it, but it was no use.

Gabriella wouldn't even look at it.

"You'll never get me into a skirt again!" she told him fiercely. "You wear it if you want! It goes with your hair."

Benedek stared at his friend, stunned. Was she making fun of him? He liked the golden locks that swept his shoulders. Should he cut them off? He had only just realised how much he hated the military-style crewcut the royal barber had always given him.

"I can wear boys' clothes, so why can't you wear girls' clothes? It won't bite!" said Gabriella, as she bundled the dress into Benedek's hands.

The dress looked amazing on Benedek, almost as if he had been altering it for himself, rather than for Gabriella. And he felt good in it too. Reluctant to bury the dress at the back of the wardrobe again, he decided he would put it on from time to time. At first, he wore it only rarely and with some trepidation, but his friends assured him he could wear it with pride any time he wanted.

One morning, when Benedek happened to be wearing the dress, Gréta dropped in on them. She brought some news: Benedek's parents and Gabriella's father were on their way to the cave. They had had enough of their children being missing and had decided to investigate the rumours that had come their way: that there had never been a kidnapping, nor a heroic death, and that the young people were living happily together in the dragon's den.

Benedek was very alarmed. His parents were coming! They would tell him off for being away for so long! And as for the dress, well, he would have to get changed immediately. What would they say if they saw it?!

"They're your parents. Shouldn't they see you as you are?" asked Gabriella, stopping him as he retreated into the cave.

It wasn't long before the royal dignitaries arrived. The dragon helped them up to the rocky peak. The parents and their children looked at each other in silence. Benedek felt

his skin burning, scalded by his mother's tears and his father's stern gaze.

"Tell me there'll be a wedding, at least!" said Gabriella's father, breaking the silence. He looked wearier than when Benedek had last seen him at the palace.

"No, there won't!" burst out Gabriella. "Benedek and Baldur are my friends. I love them to bits, but I'm not in love with either of them! When will you finally accept that I will never be in love with anyone?!"

"But if the right person—"

"There is no right person!" cried Gabriella.

Gréta went over to her ex-husband and tried to make peace. "She's happy as she is. We've no right to criticise her or force her to get married."

The king hung his head. It was clear that he had counted on getting an answer and was only now beginning to accept what he had denied for so many years.

The conversation between Benedek and his parents was taking quite a different shape. To be more precise, it wasn't taking shape at all. Benedek's mother was sobbing and hugging her son, and begging him to come home, while his father looked on wordlessly.

"I missed you so much, my little one! You've lost weight! And your hands are so rough! Come home! The palace is empty without you."

Benedek felt sorry for his parents, and he decided to return home with them. For a short time. Baldur grumbled unhappily, but he accepted Benedek's plan. Gabriella, on the other hand, flew into a passion and ran off to her room without even saying goodbye. Her behaviour did nothing to lift Benedek's spirits, and as he got into the carriage, he was already questioning his decision.

On their journey back to the palace, Benedek told his parents how he would like his new life at the palace to be different from before. He wanted to exchange the old,

hateful activities like fencing, riding and hunting for drawing and sewing. He would make toys, design clothes and keep his hair long. His mother, all smiles, promised to support him in this. Benedek could hardly wait to be able to invite his friends to visit and to be reconciled with Gabriella.

His parents kept their word. Within the confines of palace life, Benedek was able to do as he liked. But despite this, the old sadness stole back into his heart. He missed his friends, and there was something else lacking that he couldn't put into words. Perhaps it was that when he had made a new dress or finished a new drawing, no one seemed to be genuinely interested in them? Or that he didn't have a free choice of what to wear on formal occasions, only at other times? Or that when he gave a soft toy to the adults at court, they looked embarrassed and referred immediately to the children they knew? Or that he couldn't just go down to the kitchens when the fancy took him? Once, when he had plucked up the courage to do so, the cook hadn't known what to do with a royal family member who wanted to work – and bake cakes, what's more! Benedek was also having to get used to a new and rather unpleasant sensation. People were whispering behind his back: his brothers and sisters, the servants, and the ordinary people. He could never hear what they were saying – they always stopped when he turned towards them – but he sensed they were talking about him.

It was on the day of his birthday that Benedek decided he would go back to live with his friends. A banquet had been organised in his honour and, as usual, his father had instructed him to dress for the dinner in trousers, as befitted a prince. Benedek felt ashamed of himself when he was with his father. He felt almost as if he were a worse son now than when they had been fishing him out of a puddle after a gallop or a jousting match. But luckily Gabriella's protest was still ringing in his ears.

At the end of the banquet, his father reached across and gave him a beautifully crafted sword as a present. "The noblest of weapons, which gladdens the heart of every man and which he wears with pride."

Benedek's heart was not gladdened by this gift, however. This was the moment he decided, once and for all, that it was time to go home. That night he wrote a letter to Gabriella and Baldur and packed up his belongings.

But his plan was foiled before he could carry it out. In the morning, when he told his parents that he intended to leave, they locked him in his room. Guards were posted outside his door and there seemed to be no chance of escape.

Five days later, Gabriella and Baldur arrived, just as it was getting light. Baldur roused everyone in the palace with his horrible bellowing. When he and Gabriella spotted Benedek waving to them from his window, they flew up and, with a single swipe of his tail, the dragon smashed a hole in the wall.

"Couldn't manage to open a window, I see!"

Gabriella's laughter was the first thing Benedek heard as the dust settled. He had never felt so happy to see anyone. Clambering out from under the rubble, he leapt onto Baldur's back. As he hugged his friends, he was fighting back the tears. Gabriella's eyes (though she would never have admitted it) were also wet. Then they flew back home, rejoicing.

Benedek soon settled back into life at the cave. He passed the time freely and cheerfully, no longer afraid to do what he loved. In a letter to his parents, he apologised for the damage his friends had caused and invited them to visit whenever they felt like it. When they eventually did, years later, Benedek's new little family welcomed them with open arms. From then on, the families met often and with joy. And Benedek, Gabriella and Baldur lived happily ever after, loving and caring for each other as true friends do.

Judit Ágnes Kiss

Róza Goes to the Ball

Once upon a time, there lived a little girl called Róza. She loved her parents very much and they in turn doted on her. Her mother and father sat her on their lap and stroked her when her tummy hurt and told her stories every night before she went to sleep.

One day, however, her mother disappeared, and when Róza looked for her, she was told that she had died. Róza missed her terribly, but as time went by she found she could no longer remember what her mother had looked like. It was no use looking at her photograph, she didn't recognise the face on it. Still, she was certain that one day her mother would return to console her.

Her father, however, seemed inconsolable. He barely spoke to Róza and drank frequently from a big bottle that he

never shared with her. When he did this, he would start crying and fall asleep in his clothes. Róza would have to change into her pyjamas all by herself and tell herself a story as she lay alone in the dark.

One day, a lady turned up at their house. She looked nothing like Róza's mother. She had a little son and a little daughter of her own, but she still looked nothing like Róza's mother. Róza's father was happy to have the lady with them, and while Róza did try her best to be happy too, she couldn't.

The lady and her children lived with them for a while, but she paid no attention to Róza, and Róza learned how to cook for herself and how to wash her own clothes, and she continued to tell herself a story at night.

Eventually, the lady moved out, taking her children with her, and Róza and her father were left by themselves. Although there were two of them, Róza was still alone. She got up alone in the mornings, made herself breakfast, packed her bag, and went off to school by herself. When she came home in the afternoons, she was alone. She cleaned the house and tidied up, washed the clothes and hung them out as if she were her own mother. When she made dinner, she always buttered a piece of bread for her father too. Her father ate it, but never said thank you. Róza was sure he was grateful to her though. In the evening, in the dark, she would tell herself a story, and in her mind she was telling it to her father as well, and she hoped he could hear it, even if he wasn't nearby.

One day, the whole school was a-buzz with the news that there would be a masquerade ball. Róza had nothing beautiful to wear to a ball. The other children often laughed at her because her clothes were stained or had holes in them, were too tight or hung loosely off her. Still, Róza was determined. She would go to the ball.

That afternoon Róza was alone again at home. She wondered how she could get hold of a ball gown. Could she sew one for herself from the worn, greying lace curtains in the living room? She barely knew how to sew – all she had learned to do was sew buttons back on when they came off. She picked up a stool and was taking it into the living room to stand on as she unhooked the curtains, when suddenly she heard a great crash.

The wardrobe door had fallen off!

Róza took the stool, climbed onto it and tried to put the door back on its hinges. Just then, she noticed something white lying on the top shelf of the wardrobe, wrapped in thin tissue paper. She took it out carefully and unwrapped it. Inside the paper was a beautiful, snow-white dress. Róza recognised it immediately. It was her mother's wedding dress. A framed photo of her wearing it hung on the wall in the hallway.

Róza's heart began to pound. Wherever her mother was now, she had sent her this dress! Róza put it on right away. It was a little long, reaching all the way to the ground, and a little loose around the waist, but Róza had a wide, gold-coloured silk ribbon which she tied around her waist to pull the dress in. She pinned up the hem by an inch or two and looked at herself in the mirror, turning this way and that as she did so. The dress was truly lovely.

"Thank you, Mother!" she whispered.

When Róza told herself a story that night, she felt that her mother was with her and that it was really her telling it.

When she got up the next morning, Róza made breakfast for herself and buttered a slice of bread for her father. She put the coffee on to brew because her father had come home late the night before, and the bottle he liked to drink from was empty again. When this was the case, a coffee usually did him good. Róza packed herself a sandwich to eat at morning break, and made one for her father, who was still sleeping. Then she set off for school.

She was in a good mood.

The other children even remarked on it, saying, "Having a good day, Róza?"

The ball was on Saturday, and Róza spent the whole day preparing for it. She made a mask for herself and hid her hair under a colourful silk scarf. She put on the white wedding dress and looked in the mirror. Róza didn't recognise herself and was sure no one else would either. She changed back into her ordinary clothes and packed the dress, the mask and the scarf into a bag to take with her.

When Róza arrived at school, the ball was already underway. No one noticed her. She slipped into the nearest toilets and got changed. She had no dancing shoes, but she didn't want to wear her trodden-down trainers – there was a chance someone might recognise them! She ran into the ballroom barefoot. All eyes turned towards her, and none them of lit up in recognition. Many of the others were in masks, but Róza was the only one who had managed to completely conceal who she was. Everyone was curious about her, but if they spoke to her, she didn't reply and only shook her head. She did not allow anyone to come close enough to pull off her mask. Boys and girls approached her, all wanting to dance with her and solve the mystery, but Róza kept quiet and danced in silence with whoever asked her.

At the end of the evening, the king and queen of the ball were chosen.

Róza knew the king of the ball only by sight. He was older than her, and every girl in school had a crush on him. For queen of the ball, most of the guests chose the mysterious, masked princess. Róza went up onto the stage and smiled under her mask. No one could see her do it. They placed a crown on her head and clapped as she and the king paraded down the room hand in hand and started the final waltz together.

"Now will you tell me who you are?" asked the king of the

ball, but Róza just shook her head. When the boy reached towards her face to lift off her mask, Róza pulled away from him and ran off. She felt a splinter go into her foot, but she kept running, all the way to the toilets.

There she took off the dress and put her old clothes back on. She hid the crown under her coat so that no one would see it, and limped home in her trodden-down trainers, her foot hurting from the splinter.

At home, she found her father stretched out on the kitchen floor, snoring and still clutching the empty bottle. Róza carefully laid a blanket over him and placed a pillow under his head before going to the bathroom.

She took another look at herself in the bathroom mirror. She was in her usual old clothes, but in the mirror she saw the queen of the ball. Her feet were black with dirt, and it was only when she gave them a good clean that she saw the splinter that had worked its way under her skin. She took out her sewing needle – the one she used to sew buttons back on, the one she would have used if she had sewn herself a dress from the curtains – and started to work the splinter free. She took a deep breath, gritted her teeth and with one big tug, managed to get it out. Carefully, she wrapped her mother's dress back up in the white tissue paper and hung it up in the wardrobe. She put on her nightdress and laid the crown beside her on her pillow.

When she told herself a story that night in the dark, again Róza felt like her mother was speaking to her. She was sure her father could hear it too, even if he was snoring on the kitchen floor with an empty bottle in his hand. She knew that, whatever happened, she was now a queen, and her mother would always come back to her when she needed comfort.

Noémi Rebeka Horváth

Little Lina's Big Adventure

Once upon a time there was a very little girl. Some said the reason she was so tiny was because her house on the edge of the town was smaller than small. Others said that her father was the king of the dwarves, Kapanyányimonyók himself. But don't you believe the half of it!

Like every tiny thing, little Lina was born from a flower, and not from just any flower – from a stunningly beautiful rose. Her family were overjoyed at the baby's arrival and they cherished and pampered her. People came from miles around to marvel at the child's glossy black hair, her chestnut-brown eyes and her sun-kissed brown skin. They thought she was a real little miracle. A little one because, even when she was older, she could still sleep quite comfortably in a bed made from a walnut shell.

Lina may not have grown any bigger as she got older, but she did have an enormous amount of love in her heart. She was too small to feed the family's dog – as she couldn't even reach into its bowl – but she found other ways to care for the creatures around her. She would get up before sunrise and climb up to the top of the big walnut tree in the garden to give dew to the little swallow chicks to drink. She loved being with them because the young birds were nearly as small as she was. She was always busy, and people said of her that you never saw that tiny girl twiddling her thumbs. If she wasn't crouching in the swallows' nest, then she was helping her mother or coming to the aid of animals that were in trouble: beetles, snails and teeny-tiny fleas. For Lina knew that even the tiniest creatures were important. She had learned that from the books her father read to her in the evenings. Lina knew them by heart, every one.

One evening, however, a new storybook came into her hands.

"Li-na the Fai-ry," she said, spelling out the words on the cover. "Lina the Fairy!" The little girl dropped onto her walnut-shell bed in surprise. "This is the story I'd like today!"

An indulgent smile crept over her father's face. "Her story is a very special one. Only the most special little girls are allowed to hear it." His rough-skinned fingers smoothed the surface of the page. "Real *big-little* girls!"

Hearing this, Lina hung her head. She would never be big, – and maybe not even *after* never. "Well, then . . . I don't want to hear it, after all," she mumbled. "Big . . . I'll never be big, Papa! Never, never. It's impossible."

"Nothing's impossible! And only the truly great are great enough to be small," smiled her father. Then he began to read the story.

"Once upon a time there was a fairy king. He was a tiny little fairy king, but his kingdom was bigger than any mortal has ever seen! He had a son too, about the same age as you, but the king couldn't find a wife for him anywhere in all the seven lands. The old king decided, therefore, that every marriageable fairy girl would have to complete a task:

"'If any one of you fine princesses can hide so well that my son cannot find you, you will be Prince Klaus's bride. But beware! If my son discovers a princess's hiding place before the time is up, she will forfeit all hope of a reward.'

"The king's heralds carried this announcement far and wide, and many girls put on their finest gowns and their smartest shoes for the occasion. Soon they were lining up in the fairy king's palace, glittering with jewels and silks and satins.

"Three days and three nights later, the king began to count. 'One, two, three! When I open my eyes, let there be no girl in sight!'

"And – *whoosh!* – the girls scattered so fast that by the time the king opened his eyes again, the girls had vanished. Fairy princesses were tucked behind every pillar, and more were hidden away on every floor of the palace. The young prince started to look for them. Some were no trouble to find: they were crouching in the burrows of toads and in mouse holes. Others were more difficult. But even so, it wasn't long before their sparkling shoes caught the prince's eye. The girls who had been discovered left the palace despondent, more of them with every hour.

There were still plenty to be found however."

Lina's father's small fingers quickly flipped a few pages of the book.

"And unless the princesses have crept out since then,

the prince is probably still looking for them!"

Little Lina's eyes grew wide. *What on earth . . .* "Is that the end, Papa?" She couldn't believe it.

"Yes, my little one," said her father, as he stood up to put the book back on the shelf (after all, the book needs a place to rest at night too). "That's the end of the story."

"But it can't be!" cried Lina, more puzzled than ever and very wide awake indeed. "A story can't end like that!"

"It can't?" asked her father, hiding a smile. "Well then, how should a story end?"

"With dancing!" cried his daughter, leaping to her feet and twirling around twice with her pillow in her arms. "With lots of dancing! And with adventures! And with palaces that turn round on dogs' legs!"

This made them both laugh, as, in their land, children knew the stories of Baba Yaga, a witch who lived in a spinning palace on top of a duck's leg.

"There are some stories we have to finish ourselves," said Lina's father as he sat her back down on her bed, then gently tucked her up. "Sleep tight, little Lina!"

Although Lina had not been tired a moment before, she fell fast asleep as soon as she laid her head on the pillow. And she dreamed about dancing and adventures and palaces spinning on dogs' legs.

The next day Lina made a big announcement. "I'm going on a big adventure today, Mama!" she boasted, jumping down from her chair.

As you can see, Lina wasn't very good at keeping secrets. Secrets were good, she thought, if everyone knew them and they could all enjoy them together.

"A big adventure?" asked her mother, amazed. "What kind of big adventure?"

"One with dancing and daring feats and a palace spinning on a dog's leg!" Lina told her eagerly.

Hearing this, her mother's eyes grew wide. "That's a lot of

adventure for just one day!"

"I need to help the fairy king!" said Lina, giving her mother a wave as she ran out of the door. "I can't leave him to find all those princesses by himself!"

That was a big enough job for two tiny people, let alone one!

Lina set off for the local shop, thinking she had seen a lot of toads there, up on the sweet shelf.

Two great leaps took her over the threshold.

"Yes, little one?" The shopkeeper adjusted her spectacles in astonishment. "May I help you?"

"I'm looking for toads!" explained Lina. "Lots and lots of toads that might be helping fairy princesses to hide."

The woman's eyes grew bigger. "Ah, I think I can help you with that," she smiled, and lifted Lina up.

She took two steps to the left then three to the right. "Was it these kinds of toads you were looking for?"

Those were exactly the kind of toads Lina was looking for! There they were, lined up on the shelf like soldiers.

"Yes, yes!" she cried, jumping down among them.

She went along the line, asking each and every sugar toad, "Have you seen a princess, by any chance, sir? And you, madam? You can tell me! I'm good at keeping secrets!"

But the sugar toads did not seem very talkative, so in the end, Lina turned to the shopkeeper crossly. "But – where can the princesses be?"

"Hmm . . ." The shopkeeper looked all along the shelves of sugary treats, then gave a laugh. "A-ha! The answer is simple!" She bent down to the tiny girl conspiratorially and whispered, "If a princess kisses a frog or a toad, he turns into a super-handsome prince! Perhaps all the princesses that were hiding here have found their prince!" The shopkeeper smiled.

Lina was very pleased by this answer. She gave a loud laugh. "The princesses hid away . . . but then *they* were the

ones doing the finding!" she chuckled. "That's funny!"

The shopkeeper helped Lina back to the door. "This must be a fun game! But why are you looking for princesses, little one?"

"It's a secret, so I'll tell you," said Lina with a solemn nod. "I'm helping the fairy prince to find them. But if they aren't here . . ." She pondered for a moment. "You don't happen to know where the mice live? I'm looking for really little ones!"

The tiniest little mice? the shopkeeper thought to herself. Then she opened the door for Lina. "They're at the toy shop! Right over there! That's where the tiniest little mice live!"

"Thank you! I'd better get going! And take care of the toads!"

Lina ran on, straight towards the toy shop, which was owned by an old man. She pulled up short at the threshold, cleared her throat and knocked on the door. She didn't need to wait long. The shopkeeper may have been old, but his hearing was sharper than a baby rabbit's.

Bending down to the ground, he adjusted his huge spectacles. "Well, hello, young lady! How can I help you?"

"I'm looking for really small mice," said Lina, making herself as tall as she could. "Can you help me?"

The old man's eyebrows shot up as far as his white hair, but he nodded. "I believe I can, my dear!" He ushered her into the shop, then pulled out a big chair. "Up there!" he said, pointing to the topmost shelf. "They're up on that shelf, hiding from the paper eagles!"

The old man climbed up carefully and placed Lina in among the many toy mice.

The mice looked at the little girl with their big, black button eyes. "Hello, mice!" she said, stepping closer. "I'm looking for some fairy princesses who are hiding. Will you help me find them? Please, little mice!"

The mice, however, said nothing and just carried on staring at her.

"Fairy princesses in hiding?" said the old man, scratching his head. "I wonder . . ."

He glanced over at the nutcrackers suspiciously, then bowed to Lina and went on in a very low voice. "Those princesses aren't here any longer, I'm certain of it." He nodded solemnly and tipped his head towards the nutcrackers. "Those chaps over there are all fine, upright soldiers." He turned towards them and saluted. "If they had seen any fairy princesses wandering about, they would definitely have escorted them back home."

"Oh," said Lina. She let the old man help her down. "That's very good of them."

"I'm sorry, young lady," said the old man, pushing up his spectacles. "If I see a princess, I'll let you know."

"Thank you."

Lina shuffled out of the shop, downcast. She saw that the sun was going down. Oh no! Every little girl should be home by teatime. Even the big-little ones!

Lina ran, her hair flying out behind her, all the way to her own front door. But when she got there, she froze. She hadn't been able to help anyone that day, and she felt bad. What if there were still some princesses hiding, and the prince couldn't find them without her? A tear rolled down her cheek.

"Miss?"

A stranger came up to her. His small, green eyes were full of concern. "What is wrong? Who's been upsetting you?"

With a single sweep, the stranger pulled out his sword. It was the size of a pin and glinted golden in the rays of the setting sun.

"I'll protect you, miss!" he cried, swishing his sword a couple of times. "Don't cry!"

Lina looked up, sniffing, and was so surprised at what she saw that she fell over backwards and landed on her bottom. It was the prince! The brave fairy prince himself,

who was just as little as Lina.

"Why? Who are you?" she asked.

"Forgive my rudeness." The boy stuck his sword in the soft earth and bowed. "Klaus at your service, Prince of the Spring That Is and Isn't To Come." He looked up. "And to whom do I have the pleasure of speaking?"

"Lina . . . I mean . . ." She dusted herself off and straightened her skirt. It seemed to have grown a bit bigger since the start of the day. Not only her skirt, but all of her. "Thumbelina!"

The prince smiled then burst out laughing.

"What's so funny?" asked Lina, folding her arms crossly.

Well, look at that! Lina's arms had grown as large as big people's arms!

But Lina was more bothered by being laughed at.

"It's your name!" The prince came closer. "Why isn't your name Lina the Fairy?"

"Because . . ." The little girl had to think about it. "Because I'm not a fairy!"

"I suppose you're not a princess either?" said the boy. "As it happens, I'm seeking out princesses who are hiding, and you seem to be the last of them." He smiled. "You did a really good job, I must say!"

Lina's brown eyes widened, and her face went as red as the rose that she was born from. "But I . . . You see . . . I . . . I wasn't hiding! But—" She glanced around quickly to see if there was anywhere suitable nearby. "I could go and hide now!"

"No!" Prince Klaus caught her gently by the arm. "Don't go off and hide again! I've been looking for you all my life, and I don't want to have to do it all over again. Please, don't ever hide from me again."

"I–I didn't hide from you," explained Lina. "I just . . . I'm just small. People don't notice me."

"I noticed you." The prince stood tall, then his shoulders

sagged. "Maybe . . . maybe you don't like me in that way?"

Well, that was not the case at all, of course! The prince was the super-duper most handsomest prince that Lina could imagine. Even the most beautiful princess would not have been lovely enough for him.

"Oh no! It's not that . . . I just have things to do, helping the little creatures – all of them."

The prince looked at her thoughtfully. "You know best," the boy said. "But as a fairy queen you would be able to help everyone."

A smile crept over Lina's face.

"And you could be my queen!"

Being able to help *every* little creature, that was what Lina had always dreamed of. Helping those who were in trouble and those who might end up in trouble . . . Now that she was big, she would be able to look after even more animals. And she really *was* big!

"Greatness is not about being tall and strong . . ."

Just then Lina's father appeared, a secretive smile playing on his lips. "The true measure of greatness is how much love you have in your heart." He closed the book that was still open in his hands. "You've grown up, Lina."

She had?

Lina took a good look at herself. So this was what it felt like to be big!

Sára Harka

Kitti and Karola

Kitti had always loved to press her nose to the windowpane and look out at the town of Boldogliget: the lavender-tinted hills, the babbling stream and the ancient, twisted cherry tree on the cobbled square. She liked watching the children running around, flying kites up on the hillside or helping themselves to cherries from the tree. Between her language lessons and her piano practice, she would imagine herself out there playing with them.

But as the years went by and Kitti got older, Boldogliget presented an increasingly sorry sight. The trousers of the kite-flying children became ragged. In the square, mothers started begging, getting down on their knees to plead for a couple of bread rolls. One day, Kitti saw an old woman scooping up water from the dirty stream to drink.

Kitti heaved a great sigh and, taking her eyes off the old woman, cast them over her room. The drapes around her bed swayed in the breeze. New clothes hung on the doorhandle, freshly ironed. The pink silk pillow on her bed was creased, but why straighten it up when the servant would do it?

Knock, knock, went someone at her door, then without waiting for an answer, in came her father.

"Kitti, why don't you have your head in your maths book?" he asked.

Her father was a man of substance, with a substantial belly and a substantial moustache. He gripped the strap of his braces in one hand, and with the other, twisted his bristly, black moustache.

"But, Papa, it's the summer holidays!"

"And you should be doing something useful with them!"

Kitti hung her head, then the words she had held back for so long came tumbling out of her mouth. "Can I help you with your work?" she asked, blushing as soon as she had said them.

"*You* help me with my work?!" said her father, astounded.

"I'd like to be mayor one day, just like you," said Kitti, casting her eyes down. "Of course, only if that's what the townspeople want too."

The mayor's face first went pink, then grew redder and redder until it became as red as a tomato. "You? A girl? Mayor of Boldogliget? Don't make me laugh!"

"But, Papa, the town needs help!"

"Trust me, my dear. You can't help these people," he told her, stroking his moustache again. "Every day I get letters complaining that some family needs this or that, and the school needs something else . . . Nothing is ever good enough for these people!"

"But, Papa!"

"It's always 'but Papa, but Papa' with you . . . That's enough! Put this silly idea out of your head and find something useful to do!"

Her father stormed out. *Bang!* went the door behind him.

Kitti sighed. She had known her father wouldn't like her idea. If only she could convince him. She couldn't stand being in this pink room a moment longer. She had to do something!

Kitti looked out of the window. It was too high to jump out of. But maybe, if she stepped out onto the windowsill, and got hold of the branch of the cherry tree . . .

That was it! That was the way! Kitti glanced back at the door to make sure no one was coming. Plucking up her courage, she climbed out of the window. She caught hold of a thick branch and climbed onto the tree. From there it was easy to clamber down. The bark made a rip in her lace-trimmed dress, but that didn't bother her. She jumped down onto the ground from the lowest branch and brushed the dirt off her hands. She'd done it! The breeze was fresh on her face, and she felt free.

In her joy she did a twirl, and as she spun round – *bump!* – she knocked into someone.

"Can you spare a couple of coins" asked the girl. Then, looking up at Kitti's face, she went quiet.

The two girls stared at each other in astonishment. Kitti couldn't believe her eyes. It was like looking in a mirror, but a mirror that had no frame. The beggar girl looked exactly like her! She had the same brown freckles on her milk-white face, the same impossible, curly, potato-blonde hair, and the same yellow patch in the middle of her big, green eyes.

"Why do you look just like me?" whispered Kitti.

"Well, why do you look just like me?" the beggar girl retorted.

Each stared at the other, then they slowly walked around each other, gaping. Each girl examined the other from all sides and found they were identical. The only difference was that the beggar girl's hair was more tangled, her nails were dirtier, and her clothes were scruffier.

Wow! Is that what I look like from behind? wondered Kitti.

Is my nose really that pointy? thought the other girl.

Incredulous, they stared at each other, then burst into giggles. They laughed so hard they had to gasp for breath. How was this possible? And when they finally calmed down, it was enough for one of them to glance at the other, and off they went again, guffawing loudly and slapping their knees. It felt so good to laugh together under the cherry tree!

"What's your name?" asked Kitti, drying her eyes.

"Karola," the girl replied.

"Let's swap places for a day!"

Karola looked at Kitti, wide-eyed. "You mean that?"

Kitti nodded.

"I saw where you climbed down from," said Karola. "You're the mayor's daughter. I bet you get scrambled egg brought to you in bed every morning and your wardrobe is stuffed full of gorgeous dresses! Why would you want to swap places with me?"

"My room's full of lovely things, but I don't get to see anything of the world outside it," sighed Kitti.

"Let's change places then!" said Karola. "This is going to be the biggest adventure ever!"

The girls bade each other farewell. Karola climbed up the cherry tree the same way that Kitti had come down it, then scrambled in through the window.

"Wait!" Kitti shouted after her. "Make sure to scrub your nails really well and put on a clean dress!"

"And don't you forget to feed the cats," Karola called back before she disappeared behind the curtains.

Kitti strolled along to the shack on the bank of the stream where Karola and her family lived. As she stepped through the door, she noticed a musty smell. Karola's home was completely different from her own. Water was dripping into a bucket from the ceiling, and a burned-out lightbulb dangled on the wall. A mouse dashed between her feet and Kitti shrieked.

"Karola, my pet. Is that you?" came a woman's voice. *She must be Karola's mother,* thought Kitti.

"Yes, it is."

The woman was lying in bed, and although she had three layers of blankets over her, her teeth were chattering.

"Have you got a fever?" asked Kitti, putting her hand on the woman's forehead. It was burning hot.

"Yes, my pet, but I'll be better in no time," the woman replied, coughing. "Where did you get that lovely dress?"

"I–I–I found it," stammered Kitti.

"That's all right then. You're a clever girl. Please give me a hand with the washing now. Bring in the dry clothes and wash the dirty ones. Keep an eye on your brother and sister too, I don't want them wandering off again. You'll need to sweep the house as well, but hurry, because Mrs Balog is waiting for her ironing!"

Kitti nodded obediently. *A brother and sister!* She smiled to herself. *I always wanted brothers and sisters.*

Kitti washed and cleaned. She did everything she was asked to. Her new little brother and sister were always up to something, fighting with wooden swords or pulling old threadbare socks over their hands and putting on a puppet show. While Kitti hung out the clothes, the children ran to and fro under the washing line and Kitti chased them, laughing.

"Let's look at the kittens!" said the little girl, gasping for breath, her eyes shining.

They pushed through the bushes behind the house to where a ginger cat was lying in the grass with her brindled kittens pressed up against her side. The kittens were patched black, white, and ginger.

The little boy and girl crouched down to pet the kittens and then the mother cat, who expressed her appreciation by purring loudly. Kitti tried to stroke the cat too, but the animal turned her head and moved away. She preferred to climb into the little boy's lap, from where she sniffed suspiciously at Kitti.

Well, at least you know who your real owner is, thought Kitti.

Over in the mayor's house, Karola first had a wash, then marvelled at her new room. She couldn't get enough of it. She jumped on Kitti's enormous bed – *boing, boing, boing!* – then turned out her wardrobe. She pulled out one full, twirly skirt and flower-decked hat after another. She was putting on a fashion show for herself, parading up and down the room in the new clothes, when the maid looked in.

"Oh, miss!" shrieked the maid, clutching at her heart when she saw the pile of clothes Karola had flung on the floor. "The mayor says to tell you that dinner is waiting."

Karola took a wrong turn three times before she found the dining room. Above the long table hung an ornate chandelier. Karola had never seen such a big one. In fact, she'd never seen a chandelier before in her life!

At the head of the table sat the mayor. He looked her up and down with a frown. "Your nails are dirty," he remarked.

Oh no! But it felt like was I scrubbing them for ever! thought Karola.

"And your hair looks like a bird has nested in it! What have you been doing?"

"I was just in my room, reading," replied Karola, worried that her pink cheeks would give her away.

Kitti's father scrutinised Karola for a few moments then smoothed his bristly, black moustache. "Well then, *bon appétit!*" he said.

Dinner was chicken soup, then roast duck with potatoes, and for dessert there was a mouth-watering chocolate cake. Karola had second helpings of everything – and three slices of the chocolate cake. She couldn't get enough of how delicious it all was. There was a moment when her fork stopped in mid-air though, and she remembered her family. She felt guilty, feasting while her brother and sister went hungry.

"If you've finished, your French teacher is waiting for you," said Kitti's father.

Karola broke into a sweat. *What?* She'd come to feast and take it easy, not to learn French! Hadn't she left school so that she would never have to study again?

When Kitti had finished all the household chores, she went over to Mrs Balog's house, where a pile of ironing awaited her.

"Well, then! What are you waiting for?" said the mistress of the house.

Kitti stood helplessly in front of the ironing board. She had never ironed any thing in her life.

"Come on then, pick up the iron!" the woman told her.

Kitti laid the first blouse on the ironing board and ran the iron over it. The blouse looked none the better for it. In fact, it looked even more creased, so she tried again. This time she held the iron on the cloth for longer.

"Oh, my stars! You'll burn it!" shrieked Mrs Balog.

Kitti jumped back with the iron in her hand.

"See? The collar is all brown and scorched!" cried the woman. "Put it in that cupboard with the other clothes I don't wear any more."

Kitti opened the cupboard and found nine shelves piled high with clothes. Some were beaded, some had ruffles, some were printed with dots, some with stripes – and that was just the start.

"You're never going to wear these again?" she asked in amazement.

"No. I'm bored of them, and some are too tight. And this one you've ruined," she said, pointing to the blouse.

"But why don't you give them to someone else?" asked Kitti. "I'm sure plenty of people would be glad of them."

"Cheeky girl!" scolded the woman.

She swung her hand to slap Kitti, but the girl dodged her. "Get out of here! Go home and explain to your mother why you haven't been paid today!"

Kitti stumbled home, fighting back the tears. When she got back to the house, she explained in an unsteady voice what had happened.

"Never mind, my pet," said Karola's mother, stroking Kitti's hair. "We could really have done with that money, but I'll expect we'll manage somehow."

"Mama!" interrupted Karola's little brother. "The baker

has left the bread he couldn't sell by the door."

"How many loaves did he bring?"

"Two."

"Then take one over to Mrs Molnár."

"But then, there'll only be one left for us!" said Kitti.

"Mrs Molnár has five children. I have only three. Off you go, all of you!"

The children took the loaf to the neighbour. On their return, they sat down at the table and their mother lit a candle while Kitti sliced the bread. Though there was nothing to put on it, each member of the family chewed his or her own slice in grateful silence. Only Kitti made a face, but she was so hungry that she began to eat too. During dinner, the ginger cat slipped under the table and rubbed herself against Kitti's legs in the hope of a few mouthfuls. Kitti broke off the crust and threw it to her.

Kitti could hardly wait to get to bed. She had been on her feet all day and was worn out After dinner, however, she

still had to wash up and tidy the kitchen. At last, feeling somewhat dizzy, she lay down next to the little boy and girl. The three of them slept cuddled up together in the small bed, which didn't seem such a bad arrangement to Kitti.

The next morning, as she left the house, Kitti kissed Karola's mother and siblings on the cheek. They were puzzled at the big farewell. Then she walked home across the cobbled square and climbed up the cherry tree into her room. She ran straight to the wardrobe and pulled out all her old trousers, T-shirts and coats.

Karola stuck her head out from under the pink quilt, stretched and blinked at Kitti.

"Look here, this is for you – and this. And this is for your little sister," said Kitti, throwing the clothes onto the bed. "You can take my old toys to your sister and brother too, and you know what? Take some books as well!"

Karola looked at her, startled.

"We could organise a huge collection!" went on Kitti. "Everyone from the town could bring clothes and things they don't need any longer but other people could still use. I could collect it all, and you could share it out."

"That's a fantastic idea!" said Karola, her eyes shining.

That day, the two girls put up posters all over the town telling people about the collection, then Kitti went round to her wealthy neighbours. Many of them were welcoming and happy to help.

Then Kitti visited Mrs Balog, whose ironing she had done the day before.

"Good afternoon. I am the mayor's daughter," said Kitti.

"Well, hello, my dear," said the woman, smiling at her. "What brings you round our way?"

"We're organising a collection for the poor. Perhaps you have a few clothes you don't wear any longer that you'd like to donate?"

"Why would I do that?" retorted the woman, the oily

smile vanishing from her face.

"Your neighbours have given us so much," coaxed Kitti. She bent closer and said, "Mrs Papp has donated a whole box of shoes, for example. People are saying she's the most generous woman in the town."

"The most generous, eh?" hissed Mrs Balog. "You come in now, and I'll give you a whole wardrobe-full!"

The collection was a great success, donations arriving by the sackload. The girls gathered a huge number of clothes, toy cars, jigsaw puzzles, dolls and other playthings, and Karola distributed them among the poorer families. There was a shoe for every bare foot, a storybook for every child.

Towards evening, the two girls lay on the enormous four-poster bed in Kitti's room, laughing and telling each other about the events of the day before.

"I'm going to go back to school in the autumn," Karola announced. "That French lesson was really good."

Knock, knock!

Both girls gave a start. There was someone at the door!

"Quick!" whispered Kitti. "Get into the wardrobe!"

Karola jumped in and pulled the door closed. Now that the old dresses had gone, there was plenty of space.

"Kitti, my girl," said the mayor as he came into the room. "Letters are coming in by the dozen from the townspeople."

Kitti looked apprehensively at her father. She wasn't sure whether he was going to praise her or give her a dressing-down. "What do they say?"

"They say that my daughter has acted nobly in organising a collection, and the poor families are grateful for all the donations they have received."

Kitti grinned as her father patted her on the shoulder.

"I realise I haven't taken good enough care of our town. I haven't been giving enough attention to the problems of the people. But you, in the kindness of your heart, noticed their troubles.

I think that one day you'll make an excellent mayor!"

"Thank you, Papa!" Kitti hugged her father, her arms barely reaching around his wide middle.

"Now, let's have dinner," said her father. "Feel free to invite that girl to join us, the one who slept here last night."

"What?!" said Kitti, astonished.

"Did you think I wouldn't know my own daughter when I saw her?" laughed the mayor.

Kitti scratched her head and laughed along with her father. She had been able to help the people of the town and had managed to convince her father to take better care of them. This was everything she had wished for!

"Can the girl's family come too?" came a voice from the wardrobe.

"The more, the merrier!"

"I'll run and tell them!" Karola burst out of the wardrobe, skipped over to the window and was off down the tree before you could blink.

"Karola!" shouted Kitti. "Next time, feel free to use the stairs!"

Karola waved back and raced off towards the stream.

Kitti and her father stood side by side at the window and looked out at Boldogliget: the lavender-tinted hills, the stream that babbled through the town and the ancient, twisted cherry tree on the cobbled square.

"The view from here is magnificent!" said the mayor and put his arm around his daughter.

Kriszta Kasza

Threeodore the Three-Eared Rabbit

Not so very long ago, deep in Zephyr Forest, a strange thing happened, so strange that you may not believe a word of what I am about to tell you. But it's as true as my name is Old Tom. I'm the oldest animal in the forest: 216 years, six months and two days old, to be precise. Like my tortoise ancestors before me, it is my task to chronicle what takes place here, and you who dwell beyond the forest will now be lucky enough to hear the strangest story in my book.

Exactly eight years, six months and seven days ago (I can be sure of this because that was the day my shell got a crack in it), there was much excitement in the middle of the forest. At number 6, Carrot Street, Mama Rabbit was having her babies. This was the day that Dr Boar had predicted they would be born, and every creature in the forest had gathered for the occasion. Even the toads and the centipedes had broken off their courtship dances and were standing at their windows, watching the goings-on at the rabbits' house. They were a little anxious, but confident that all would be well.

There was plenty of to-ing and fro-ing, that was for sure. Martin the Mouse had brought along the T-shirt he liked to sleep in, in case it turned into a long night. He didn't want to miss out on any of it. And it did, as it happens, turn into a long night. The centipede family made themselves comfortable in the hollow of a rotten tree and the ladybirds set about cleaning their spots (just like you brush your

teeth before bed). The squirrels kept watch, sometimes shining their firefly lanterns in at the windows so they could report back to the others. It was easy for the snowy owl. He wasn't sleepy at all. He was just dipping into a book about a magical owl called Hedwig, when a cry rang out.

"Here's the first!"

It was the midwife, Violet the Vole. The door opened, and there she stood, delighted, lifting the little newborn rabbit up over her head, according to ancient forest tradition. Everyone breathed a happy sigh, but cheering was out of the question lest they startle the tiny kit. So they resumed their patient waiting.

All this happened again when the midwife held a second little grey infant aloft.

"It's a boy!" announced the vole with satisfaction.

Sometime later she added, "I think that's going to be all."

Noises could be heard from inside, however. An excited murmur ran through the crowd. And it really was a crowd – the ant family alone came to 323!

"Is there going to be a third?" asked a little garden spider.

By the time a loud shout broke the silence of the moonlit evening, some of the animals were already drifting home, and others had fallen asleep.

"Well, I never!" came the voice of Dr Boar.

Finally, the door opened for a third time. Violet the Vole brought out another little bundle and, somewhat hesitantly, held that one aloft too. Everyone fell silent. Only Jack the Blue Jay, always a loud-mouth, spoke up.

"But this one's got one, two, *three* ears!"

"Goodness me! It's all ears! I'll summon the Forest Council right away," said Piers the Pine Marten, who was the mayor of the forest. "Tomorrow at the crack of dawn, when the woodpecker pecks five times, everything that moves – and doesn't move" (at this point, he looked at Solly the Sloth) "must be at the Bellowing Frogs' Pool."

"Off you go now. There's nothing to see here," said Connie the Cockroach, the police officer.

"Caw, caw" said a crow, in ominous tones.

The forest creatures set off for home, whispering to each other in amazement. At 6 Carrot Street, the lights soon went out.

"I'm calling him Threeodore," said Mama Rabbit in a tired voice. (Though I too was already heading home, I could still hear every word. Tortoises are not the fastest creatures in the world, as you know.)

Well, that is how the strangest story in my book began, the story of Threeodore, the Three-Eared Rabbit. And how did it go on? Listen carefully and I'll tell you.

Dawn had barely begun to break when the animals started to flock to the Bellowing Frogs' Pool (frogs really aren't quiet animals). Dragonflies darted about directing the traffic: "Crickets to the right, ants to the left! Crows to the seventh floor of the Great Willow Tree! Squirrels to the Walnut Waiting Hall! Snails to the carpark!" and so on.

At last, the dignified figure of Piers the Pine Marten came into view. The mayor got straight down to business. "Something unheard of has happened in our forest. Nothing like it has ever been recorded in a single one of our ancient chronicles. As I'm sure you are now all aware, among the new offspring of Simon the Rabbit and his family is a three-eared child! If news of this gets out, it won't be long before one of the *Daily Commotion*'s scribblers turns up here and writes something awful about our forest."

Then, to everyone's amazement, Solly the Sloth, who usually slept through these meetings, spoke up. "If I may, Mr Mayor, I would like to point out that there *is* an entry in the chronicles about something like this."

"Entry? What kind of entry? Where did you get that idea?" asked the mayor, impatiently.

"Well, as a child I used to be a bit of a layabout. In between naps, I often peeked into the *Sloth Encyclopedia of Columbia*, and I remember it mentioned something like this. What I mean is, there are unusual animals, ones who are different from the rest of us. According to the *Encyclopedia*, in countries far from here, there are animals that change their colour, and enormous giants with great big trunks." (Here a low murmur could be heard.) "Imagine – in another book I even read about a horribly ugly duckling who changed into a swan when he came of age! Why shouldn't there be three-eared rabbits too?"

"Come now. These are all just made up! What proof do we have that such animals exist, beyond an old book this sleepwalker claims to have seen?"

"I've seen all kinds of things, for that matter," the sloth went on. "As you know, I'm not from these parts. If I hadn't been left here by a travelling circus, you wouldn't believe that *I* existed. Where I come from, everything is different."

"That doesn't mean it's better! For example, what are you any good for?" hissed Sarina the Snake.

"If you ever paid me any attention, you might find out," muttered Solly.

"Let's get back to the question in hand," said Piers the Pine Marten. "I propose that we take a vote on what should happen to this kit. Next week the goshawks will be here on their usual mouse hunt. We could offer this little creature up to them."

"B–b–but, p–p–please . . ." stammered Anton the Ant, who agreed with Solly. "Why is this little newcomer so dangerous? S–s–strange things have already happened in the forest. And in our own w–w–way, we are all unusual."

"I have spines, for example," said Henrik the Hedgehog in a timid whisper.

"And I carry my house on my back," argued a snail.

"Enough!" shouted the mayor. "Let's take a vote. All those

in favour of letting the rabbit stay?"

The animals put up their paws, wings, forelegs or feelers. Only a family of rats and Sarina the Snake voted to get rid of Threeodore.

Piers the Pine Marten announced the result. "Animals! Taking into account the votes cast, the following decision has been reached: although this rabbit kit is odd-looking, he is not dangerous – for the time being. After exactly seven full moons, we will return to the question. Until then, he may live among us. But outside of Zephyr Forest his existence will be kept a secret."

The mayor closed the meeting and walked off.

So it happened that little Threeodore was saved from the goshawks and given a chance to live in the forest like any other young animal.

Time went by. The forest creatures would look sideways at Mama Rabbit when they saw her out pushing her little ones along in the pram, and Threeodore's three little ears happened to poke out from under the blanket. A few years later, when he started school, Threeodore's classmates gave him similar looks.

During the day, Threeodore played happily with the others, but in the evenings he would sometimes catch sight of his reflection in the mirror and feel sad.

"Mum, why am I different from the others?" he would ask.

"You're special, my pet!" replied Mama Rabbit.

"But the other children make fun of me. They whisper, but I can still hear them with all three of my ears. They call me 'Propellor-Ears' and 'One-and-a-Half-Wit', but I don't feel like I'm different from them!"

"Don't listen to them; listen to yourself. One day they'll realise that you're no different from them. You'll see. A rabbit should not be judged by the way he looks, but by what he does."

And one fine day, Mama Rabbit was proved right.

Night had fallen on the forest, and all was quiet. Only Threeodore lay awake, twisting and untwisting his little ears in an effort to get to sleep. He couldn't stop wondering why he had been blamed for knocking some plates off a shelf at school that day, rather than Chrissy the Crow, who was really the one responsible for it.

"Threeodore must have swept them off with his ears!" the other animals had shouted, pointing at him, and not even the teacher had stood up for him.

After a while, he'd had enough of this unhappy tossing and turning. "I think I'll hop around in the garden for a bit," he decided.

He got out of bed and unbolted the door. He had just got to the little bench at the end of the garden, when some strange sounds reached his ears (all three of them). He could hear snapping, crackling and sizzling. From far away, something seemed to be approaching the forest.

Threeodore dashed into the house and tried to wake his father. "Dad! Dad! Wake up! I can hear something and it's getting louder!"

Papa Rabbit clambered out of bed and went over to the door, shivering. "Ugh, my boy, it's as dark as a raven's breast and cold as a frog's head out there! What are you doing up? I can't hear anything. Stop worrying and go to sleep. If anything was wrong, Connie the Cockroach would have sounded the alarm," he said, then went back to bed.

But Threeodore couldn't stop worrying. He was trying to come to a decision. "I must believe in myself and believe in my ears!" he concluded at last and ran out of the house.

He made straight for the house where Chrissy the Crow lived. The shutters were closed, but he shouted through them.

Papa Crow's sleepy voice came back to him. "Who's there, and what do you want so late at night?"

"It's me, Threeodore! Something's wrong, I can feel it! Hear it, I mean! Something's coming and it's making

a snapping and a crackling sound. Please, fly over the forest and see what it is!"

"Very well," grunted Calvin the Crow, Chrissy's father. As a retired police officer, he had been longing for a bit of adventure.

Off he flew.

When he peered round the Great Willow Tree, he was struck dumb. Then he burst out into a wild cawing. "Fire! Fire! The reed beds next to the forest are burning. Fire at the Bellowing Frogs' Pool! Wake up, everyone!"

In the blink of an eye, lamps went on all over the forest, and it became a hive of activity. Animals started rushing about, scrambling to help. Threeodore ran over to the hunting horn the animals used in emergencies and blew it as hard as he could.

"What's going on?" said Piers the Pine Marten, startled out of his sleep. "Who blew the horn? What's happening? Is that the fire brigade, over there?"

A large number of rats had leapt into action on hearing the alarm. They had water guns and were wearing poppy-red vests. "Run! Before the fire reaches the forest! We can slow it down!" they cried and scattered in every direction.

The other animals had filled buckets with water and were running towards the blaze. They were just in time. With everyone lending a hand, the fire got smaller and smaller until, at the entrance to the forest, it went out with a big puff of smoke. It had scorched Oliver the Otter's den a little, but he'd always fancied a more rustic roof in any case.

"Hooray! The forest is saved!" cried a little mouse, and very soon everyone was joining in the cheering.

Piers the Pine Marten climbed onto a fallen tree trunk, still in his wet clothes. "Listen, animals! We have prevented a disaster, and just in time too. Who was it that alerted the authorities to the danger?"

"It was Threeodore!" shouted Chrissy the Crow, who had been watching the events from her family's nest, shaking with fear. Her father confirmed this, then told the other animals what Threeodore had done.

"That's right! If he hadn't woken us up, we'd all have perished. The squirrels had probably built a fire to roast hazelnuts and none of them noticed that the embers were still alight. The wind blew away the smoke and nobody except Threeodore heard the fire. He's got the best hearing of all of us!"

"Long live Threeodore the Three-Eared Rabbit!" shouted a stag beetle, and everyone started to cheer.

So it was that, at an Extraordinary Meeting of the Forest Council the next day, Threeodore was made an honorary citizen of Zephyr Forest and a first officer in the fire brigade. From that day forward, no one made fun of him or whispered about him behind his back. Everyone said hello to him when they met him in the forest, and they even started to take their little problems to him.

"Threeodore, would you come and listen to my stove? It's making a knocking sound. What do you think is wrong with it?"

"Please will you come and listen to what the fish are saying? They're talking about where the tastiest algae can be found."

And so on.

Solly the Sloth, who had stood by Threeodore from the beginning, was held in greater esteem after the fire. He was made a teacher of the forest animals. The little ones loved his exotic stories about Columbia, and the fact that they had several breaks a day for a siesta.

Threeodore the Three-Eared Rabbit soon became the most famous animal in the forest. Even the much-feared *Daily Commotion* had nothing bad to say about him.

But Threeodore never let all this go to his head.

One thing had changed though. When he was standing in front of the mirror washing his ears in the evening, he no longer asked his mother, "Why am I like this?"

Instead, he said, "I'm fine as I am. Just as I am, three ears and all! I am the happiest rabbit in the world!"

And that's the end of the story. All this talking has worn me out. I'm not a young reptile any more, you know!

Oh, just one more thing. I hope you don't get downhearted when you look at yourselves in the mirror. Are your ears freckly? Does your nose glow? Maybe your shell is cracked too? Don't let that bother you! It just means you're special too.

Take it from me, Old Tom, the wisest animal in Zephyr Forest.

Edina Kertész

The Twirly-Whirly Drinking Straws

The train pulled in to platform 17, the very last platform
in the very large station. It puffed and panted like an
exhausted runner. The doors opened, and a group of
children with rucksacks piled out.

A crowd of fathers and mothers, grandmothers,
grandfathers and uncles was waiting for the children,
who had been away at a forest camp. They surrounded the
children, buzzing like bees around spring flowers.

But Janó and Magda found no one waiting for them.
The others were shouting and laughing and saying goodbye,
then they gradually disappeared, walking off in ones and
twos, till only Janó and Magda were left.

Janó looked this way and that, waiting for Mum to
emerge from the crowd. A man with two big suitcases,
running for his train, nearly knocked the two children over.

Still no Mum.

"It must be that boss of hers, the one who shouts so
much. I bet he didn't let her out of the lamp factory in
time," said Janó.

Magda didn't respond. Instead she ran her fingers over
the piece of moss in her palm. The moss was silky and as
soft as a kitten's fur. She had found it on their forest hike,
on a quiet path where the trees stretched over their heads,
the leaves whispering secrets. Magda knew a secret too, one
she had never told a living soul. She was very careful not to
let it slip out by chance, not even when the camp leader had

started to sing a song about bears as they walked along. Magda had sung along, as the trees opened up and the sun stroked her face.

There was no sunlight coming through the glass roof of the station. Instead, sombre clouds were gathering overhead, and somewhere up high, dark-grey pigeons were flapping their wings.

"She's not coming," said Janó. "Let's go."

Magda put the piece of moss back in the pocket of her flowery skirt and took Janó's hand. "How do the pigeons find their way home?" she asked.

Janó looked up. "They follow the trail of crumbs. Always. But we don't need any crumbs, because I know what we need to do. Let's take the tram to the school, and Mum will be there waiting for us, for sure."

So that is what they did. They got on the yellow tram, travelled two stops and then got off. Magda held tightly to Janó's hand, so she wouldn't be swept away by the crowd. As they passed the florist, red, yellow and blue flowers bent their heads towards the children. On the corner, a dog, sitting with his master, looked at Magda with mild, chocolate-brown eyes. Magda crouched down and stroked him, and the dog licked her hand.

Janó tugged her onwards. "Come on. Mum will be getting worried."

But there was no one waiting for them in front of the school. The big blue door was locked, and the street yawned emptily.

Magda burst into tears. She couldn't help it. "Now what are we going to do? What will become of us?"

Janó scratched his head and looked around. What should they do? Where should they go? He was ashamed to find that he too was crying.

As they stood there, weeping and sniffing, an old woman in a green coat stopped and spoke to them. "What's wrong, my dears? Can't find your way home?"

Alarmed, Magda hid behind Janó. But the lady seemed so kind that, little by little, she felt braver and peeped out from behind her brother. Janó told the old lady that Mum hadn't been at the station and now they didn't know what to do.

"Come with me," said the lady, stroking Magda's face. "I'll look after you until your mother comes to get you. First, we'll go to your house and leave a message. That way, your mother will know where you are. How does that sound?"

Janó sniffed hard and tried to think. He didn't like the thought of going with this strange old lady at all. But what other choice did they have? He didn't have a better idea. He nodded and together they set off for the children's flat.

They went along the little, narrow streets, past the Chinese goods shop, the cobbler's and the rug shop, until at last they reached Janó and Magda's building. It was tall, with grimy walls and a narrow courtyard in the middle. The children lived on the far side of the courtyard.

The lady rang the bell, but no one came to the door. Mum wasn't at home and the bear wasn't answering. If the bear was at home, he was probably sleeping, as usual. Magda was glad he didn't come to the door.

That was the moment the kind lady in the green coat guessed Magda's secret, the one she had never told a soul: they had a bear living with them. A hairy, bad-tempered bear who was always either asleep or demanding that they give him something to drink because he was thirsty. Then, when he had quenched his thirst, he would fall asleep again. Mum always told them to be patient with him, but Magda was afraid of the bear because he had big paws and he sometimes used them to lash out. When he did that, she and Janó would hide under the table and stay there until the bear was asleep again.

The lady took a notebook from her bag, tore out a page and wrote in big letters:

The children are at 13 Zöldfa Street,
Second Floor, Flat 3
Aranka Zöldi, widow

Magda noticed that not only was the lady's coat green, but her name meant 'green' and she lived on Green Tree Street.

They tucked the paper behind the bars of the window, then Magda took hold of Janó's hand, and they followed the lady in the green coat back down the narrow street.

As they went along, the streets became wider, and sky appeared between the roofs of the houses. From to time, Janó would glance back over his shoulder so he could memorise the path and would know the way back.

"What are you looking at?" the lady asked him.

"Just a red sports car," replied Janó.

On they went. Janó again looked over his shoulder.

"What are you looking at?" asked the lady once again.

"I saw a black jeep, that's all," said Janó.

They passed brightly lit shop windows, among them a doughnut shop. Magda stopped. Drifting out of the shop was a mouth-watering scent of vanilla.

"Are you hungry, you two?" asked the lady in the green coat. Janó nodded. The lady went into the bakery and emerged with two large brown paper bags.

"Come on. It's not far now," she said.

Eventually they stopped in front of a huge double door. The lady took out her keys. Inside, the staircase was filled with light, and a red carpet ran up the wide steps.

"In you come, then!" smiled the lady.

Wide-eyed, Janó and Magda followed her up to the first floor, where they stopped in front of another door.

The lady opened it and ushered the children inside. The room they were standing in was airy and bright. Big, comfy armchairs stood by the windows, and a grey cat was just leaping down from one of them.

"Meet Rozina," the lady in the green coat said, as she took off her coat and hung it up on the stand. Without her coat, she seemed much smaller.

The cat came over to Magda and rubbed itself against her legs. Magda bent down and stroked her. Her coat was as soft as the moss she had in the pocket of her flowery skirt.

The cat miaowed, as if she wanted to say something. Magda bent closer and listened carefully.

"Wash your hands, my dears," said the lady, pointing to a white door.

Inside the bathroom, the water came out of a golden tap and the soap was raspberry-scented. Magda soaped her hands till they were covered in foam then wiped them on a soft, white towel. Janó just waved his hands under the tap and then reached for the towel. His hands left

a big, black mark. Magda was afraid the lady would notice, so she stuffed the towel quickly into a big wicker basket.

Back in the living room, the contents of the two paper bags were awaiting them, set on porcelain plates decorated with roses: doughnuts with coloured icing – pink, white, chocolate-striped and golden yellow.

The lady brought a jug of red-coloured squash and two tall glasses. In each of the glasses was a twirly-whirly green straw.

Magda and Janó, who felt like they could eat a horse, jumped on the doughnuts immediately. The pink ones tasted of raspberries, the yellow ones were filled with vanilla cream and the white ones were white-chocolate flavour!

The raspberry squash twisted up the twirly-whirly straws.

"I made those myself," said the lady. "The drinking-straw factory was set up by my husband, and I took it over after he died," she explained with a sad smile. The cat rubbed itself against her legs and miaowed. "Help yourselves to more doughnuts and squash, while I feed Rozina," she added, and disappeared off to the kitchen.

Janó bit into a doughnut. Magda moved closer to him and whispered, "She's a green witch, this lady."

Janó shook his head. "What are you talking about?"

"I'm telling you, she is!" insisted Magda. "Rozina told me. But there's no need to be afraid. Green witches don't harm anyone."

Janó was annoyed. "There you go again. Making up all kinds of things."

Magda wanted to reply, but just then the doorbell rang. The lady hurried to open the door.

It was the bear! He was wearing a big, grey coat and a knitted hat. "I've come for the children," he muttered.

The lady looked behind her, but the chairs the children had just been sitting on were empty.

"Well now! Where have they got to?" she said. "Wait here a minute, and I'll find them for you."

But there was no sign of Janó and Magda. The lady looked under the table, in the pantry, behind the bookshelves, even in the washing machine. They were nowhere to be found.

The doorbell rang again. This time when the lady opened the door, there was Mum, shivering and stamping her feet to get warm.

"What are you doing here?!" she asked the bear in astonishment.

"I'm taking the children," he growled.

"Oh no, you're not!" cried Mum. "I've told you, we never want to see you again."

The bear swayed towards her and lifted his great big paw to strike. Just then, there was a huge crash from the bathroom. The wicker basket tipped over, and Magda and Janó jumped out. "Leave her alone!" shrieked Magda and rushed straight for the bear.

He lashed at her, right and left. Janó and Mum couldn't just stand and watch – they flung themselves at the bear, biting and punching. The bear cried out in pain and swung his paw again.

The green witch sprang into action, whacking him hard on the head with the handle of her umbrella.

The bear roared. "You'll be sorry for this!" he growled. But, realising that they had the upper hand, he slunk out of the flat.

The door slammed behind him.

The green witch let out a great sigh. "Bless my green cotton socks!"

"I'm so sorry," said Mum. "He's the children's stepfather, you know. He kept saying he would change, and I kept on believing him. But enough is enough. He won't be bothering us again. Good riddance to him!"

Magda cuddled up to Mum, who looked down at her and

stroked her head. "I'm really sorry I was late to the station."

"Was it because of that boss who shouts so much?" asked Janó.

"No, no," said Mum, shaking her head and laughing. "I left work late because there was a party at the factory. I've been working so hard that they've decided to pay me more, and they also presented me with a huge chandelier! We'll go home and put it up, shall we? What do you say?"

"Yes, please!" cried Magda.

"Keep the straws as a memento," said the green witch, handing them to the children. "And if you feel like it, do come and visit. I'd be very happy to see you both. There will always be doughnuts!"

She winked at Janó, who started jumping for joy, springing around like a flea.

Magda took the piece of moss out of her pocket and held it out to the green witch. "If you water it, it will stay as beautifully green as it is now," she said.

And from the look on the lady's face, Magda knew she was really pleased with the gift.

Back at home, Janó and his mother put up the chandelier. Magda flipped the switch and the room filled with light, so bright it was like the sun itself was shining inside their home.

Orsolya Ruff

The Great Alfredo

Once upon a time, not so very long ago, and not so far away, there was a little boy by the name of Dani. He lived on the other side of the tower blocks, but this side of the Ladybird Nursery School. He no longer went to nursery, but he still liked to count the houses on his street every day as he walked home from school. *One, two, three . . .* Dani's family lived in the thirteenth house. He could hardly wait to get home. When he came in through the door, he would heave a happy sigh. *At last,* he would think to himself. *At last, someone will notice me.*

Dani, you see, was invisible. It wasn't that he was see-through, like the water that comes out of the tap in the bathroom. Dani was, to all appearances, perfectly ordinary, like you or me or the child next door. He had brown hair and blue eyes, and when he laughed, two little dimples would appear on his cheeks. He wasn't very tall, so when he sat at the table, he could swing his legs to and fro. He liked doing that. When he was smaller, his mother would always tell him, "Dani, don't swing your legs!" But these days, his mother was always so busy on her phone that she barely glanced up, even if Dani kicked the table leg. The other day his breakfast cereal had sloshed out onto the table, but still she had said nothing. Instead she had sighed, reached for a sponge and wiped up the milk. Her eyes had stayed on her phone the whole time.

Dani knew that he mustn't disturb his mother, because she always had a lot to do. Sometimes though, he was so unhappy that she couldn't help but notice. Then she would

muss up his hair, plant a kiss on the top of his head, and say, "Go out and play with your friends!"

Except Dani didn't have any friends.

Like I told you, Dani was invisible.

When he went out to the playground, no one came running to join him, and no one ever, *ever* invited him over to see their new toys. It wasn't that Dani was a nasty or bad-tempered child, or that he was always fighting or telling tales. He was kind and helpful, and he liked to show his toys to other children. It was simply that everyone's eyes just seemed to pass right over him.

If the teacher asked two of the children to pick football teams, he was always the last to be chosen. If the class was told to get into pairs when they were on a school outing, Dani always ended up holding the teacher's hand because there wasn't a partner left over for him.

Dani didn't mind very much, because he had figured out how to entertain himself. He always kept a little notebook and a tiny pencil in the back pocket of his trousers. When he was really bored, he would make up stories and even draw illustrations for them.

When the notebook was full, he had to look for something else to do. While the others were playing football, he would climb up the cherry tree in the school yard. This tree was so old that it no longer produced any cherries, but its branches were great for climbing. Dani would scramble up the tree like a little squirrel and stretch out on his stomach on the thickest branch. Hidden by the leaves, he would watch the children running around below. If he got bored of that, he would entice the blackbirds closer with the seeds he kept in his pockets.

At home, though, there were no blackbirds and no cherry trees. Dani lived with his mother and grandparents in a crooked little house with only a dusty yard between the narrow pavement and the house, just big enough for his

mother's little red car to squeeze into. Despite its shabby appearance, people came to their house from miles around to marvel at the climbing roses that completely covered the walls. Passers-by would become all dreamy when they smelt the scent of the yellow, white and pink flowers.

Dani wasn't interested in the roses, but he often found himself thinking about the neighbour's lime tree. This tree shaded their yard, making it pleasantly cool in summer, but Dani's mother had told him that on no account was he to climb it, even though the neighbour had often said he could.

"I wouldn't mind climbing it myself," joked the neighbour, "if it wasn't for my old bones!"

But Mother shook her head at Dani, who shrugged his shoulders resignedly.

"Go in and see your grandfather instead. He hasn't seen you for ages," said his mother.

At this suggestion, Dani felt a lead weight settle in his stomach. Dani's grandfather lived in a room right at the back of the house. Dani didn't know how old he was, maybe a hundred, possibly a hundred and ten. He was very, very old. His face was all wrinkly. He had a small, pink, knobbly nose and a puff of white hair on each side of his head. Dani had never seen him out of his bed. The old man always had the covers pulled right up to his nose, his liver-spotted hands resting on his chest. When Dani said hello, his grandfather never even twitched an eyelid.

In the beginning, Dani had told the old man jokes, but he never got so much as a smile in return. In fact, his grandfather never seemed to notice Dani was there. His eyes were always fixed on the white wall opposite, though there was nothing interesting to see. Dani had once gone over with a magnifying glass, hoping to come across some kind of secret sign, but he hadn't found anything, not even a boring old crack. Dani had come to the conclusion that his grandfather must be sleeping with his eyes open and

dreaming so deeply that he might never wake up.

When he told his mother this, she told him to stop talking such nonsense. But when he asked her what had happened to his grandfather, she never gave him a proper answer, burying her nose in her phone instead.

As for his grandmother, she just shook her head and went on arranging roses in a vase. She cut some off the wall every day, and by the next morning there would be new ones in their place, even bigger and brighter than before. You couldn't move near his grandfather's bed for all the roses, and although the room was aired regularly, their heavy, stifling scent hung over everything.

It was pretty boring being with his grandfather, so if no one was watching, Dani would slip out quietly and go nowhere near the room for days. One day, he had just made his escape when he noticed that someone had left the trapdoor to the attic open. He glanced around. The house was silent. His mother had gone to the post office, and his grandmother was gossiping with the neighbour. Dani pressed himself to the wall, then, keeping his eyes on the trapdoor, he scrambled up the narrow stairs.

Dust floated in the shafts of light filtering in between the roof tiles. Dani stepped further in, placing his feet cautiously. He ducked his head just in time to avoid walking into a crossbeam. There was a lightbulb hanging from the beam. Where could the switch be? As he stepped to the side, Dani lost his balance and the world flipped upside down.

Dani had fallen hard, but luckily he had not banged his head. Only his shoulder ached where he had fallen against a striped trunk.

Wincing, Dani rubbed his shoulder, but his curiosity was greater than his pain. He ran his eyes along the rafters until he spotted the switch. Getting slowly to his feet, he climbed onto the trunk, stood on tiptoe and reached up high.

Click!

The contents of the attic came dimly into view. His eyes fell on some old clothes, a wardrobe with a mirror on the door, a broken rocking-horse and a painting covered by a sheet.

Dani wasn't interested in the clothes. The mirrored wardrobe looked boring, and the rocking-horse seemed beyond rescue. However, he was drawn to the painting as if by a magnetic force. He climbed down off the trunk, went over to the picture and reached out his hand. He paused before pulling off the sheet. What would he find underneath? A rare and valuable painting the world would marvel at? A secret map that would lead to him to real treasure? He took a deep breath and pulled away the dusty sheet.

What he saw underneath took his breath away. It wasn't a painting nor was it a map. It was a poster of the kind you could see on the street. Just that this poster was really old. Maybe a hundred years old. It read:

Alfredo's Circus
The Greatest Show on Earth
Clowns, lions, dazzling acrobatic feats
and the World's Strongest Man
Come one, come all!

In the middle of the poster stood a man in a top hat with a twisted moustache and a splendid rose sticking out of his waistcoat pocket. He had a hoop of fire in one hand and was scratching a lion under the chin with the other.

Dani gazed at the man, entranced. It must be Alfredo, he thought. But how did this poster end up in their attic?

Just then, his eyes fell on the stripy trunk. The paint had peeled off in patches as big as your hand, but it was still a fine-looking thing. There was a padlock on it, but when he took it in his hand, it slipped open, almost of its own accord.

Dani took a big breath. What if a mouse jumped out when he lifted the lid? He smiled to himself. Well, at worst he'd get a pet. He opened the lid cautiously.

There was no mouse in the trunk. It was packed so full of stuff, nothing could be living inside it. The first thing Dani pulled out was an old red tailcoat, just like the one the Great Alfredo was wearing on the poster. *How did this get here?* Dani wondered. He felt an irresistible urge to try it on.

The sleeves were a little long, and it gave off a sharp smell, but wearing it made Dani feel like a different person. He ran his fingers lightly over the tarnished gold buttons, then went back to the trunk, curious to see what else was inside.

The next thing he pulled out was a juggling club, then another and another. Four in total. He twirled them in his fingers, but he couldn't keep even one of them in the air; he kept on dropping them. Still, this didn't dampen his curiosity, and he delved into the trunk once again.

Suddenly Dani froze. What was that soft stuff? Had he reached into a mouse's nest? He felt around more carefully, and realised it was an old wig. He gave it a good shake to get the dust out, put it on his head and stood in front of the mirror. He gave a loud laugh.

Just then, he thought he heard a noise from below. He clapped his hand over his mouth and hurried back to the trunk. He soon found a red clown's nose to go with the wig and a single turned-up clown's shoe. At the very bottom of the trunk lay a broken whip – and underneath that lurked a coiled snake!

Dani's heart was in his mouth. If the snake moved, that would be the end of him. *Finito!* The snake lay there, motionless. Dani picked up the clown's shoe and, reaching up, used it to dislodge a roof tile and let in more light. He let out a sigh of relief: what he'd thought was a snake turned out to be just a rope, the kind acrobats use for a tightrope. Dani ran his fingers gingerly over the rope, then

heaved it out of the trunk.

The trunk was empty – almost. At the very bottom was
a small book. Dani picked it up and held it to the light.
He saw that it was actually a photo album, full of old black-
and-white pictures. The photos had scalloped edges and
showed the daily life of Alfredo's circus. In one picture,
a fire-eater was holding a flaming torch in the air. In
another, a knife-thrower was aiming his knives at a pretty
woman. He never hit her, of course; the knives always
landed right next to her. Dani liked the animal photos best.
In one, horses with feathered plumes on their heads were
trotting in a circle. In another, a cute little dog was rolling
a ball along. Dani was enthralled at the sight of a lion
leaping through a hoop of fire, and in one of the photos
there was even a wrinkly elephant, carrying the world's
strongest man on his back, waving merrily to the
applauding crowd. The strongman's muscles bulged under
his sailor-stripe vest. Dani fingered his own muscles
through his sweater and resolved to do some push-ups in
the yard that afternoon.

In the final photo, the Great Alfredo himself was standing
in the centre of the ring. Behind him, the lion posed sleepily
while the dog chased the clown. Dani peered at the photo,
then frowned and flipped back through the album. There
could be no doubt about it: the Great Alfredo was none other
than the strongman – the one flexing his muscles as he sat
on the elephant's back. The Great Alfredo was not just the
circus manager, but also the lion tamer and the strongman
all rolled into one! And who knew what else . . .

Without noticing, Dani began to stroke the picture.
He felt somehow connected to this glittering world he had
never seen before. He pressed the photo album to his chest.

Just then, the dust around him lifted and started to swirl.

Dani looked about him in confusion, half expecting to see
the Great Alfredo himself step out of the shadows . . .

Instead of the top-hatted circus manager, he saw his grandmother's eyes flashing in the dark. "How many times have I told you, Dani?" she began to scold. Then she stopped mid-sentence, staring at her grandson, open-mouthed.

Dani glanced at the mirror on the wardrobe. He looked pretty strange, it was true. The wig had slipped sideways, and the sleeves of the red tailcoat hung limply over his hands. He felt himself go red, right to the roots of his hair.

"Gran, I–I—" he stammered, then, without waiting for a reply he dashed past his grandmother and out of the attic.

At the bottom of the stairs, he bumped into his mother, who clapped her hands together in astonishment. Dani didn't stop. He ran, as if someone was chasing after him, and when he reached safety, he slammed the door behind him.

He leaned against it and let out a big breath.

It was only then that he realised he had run into his grandfather's room. As usual the old man was examining something invisible on the wall. Dani knew that his grandmother and his mother would be there any minute. He knew they would give him a hard time for going up to the attic and trying on those old things. But a kind of magical force was pulling him towards his grandfather's bed. As he got closer, he knocked over a vase. The dried-up flowers fell all over the floor, but Dani paid no attention because something odd was happening.

The old man had shifted his gaze from the wall to Dani. His inscrutable dark eyes first stared blankly at him, then they seemed to come to life.

Dani looked down. "I look stupid, don't I?" he said.

There was no reply. To Dani's amazement, his grandfather lifted his wrinkled, veined hand and ran his fingers over the tailcoat's tarnished golden buttons.

"Well, well, the old coat," sighed the old man.

Dani went very still. "You've seen this coat before?"

The old man closed his eyes for a moment, then gave

a wan smile. "Seen it? I've worn it!"

Dani swallowed quietly. It was then that he realised he was still clutching the photo album. He sat down carefully on his grandfather's bed and opened the album, turning to the photograph of the Great Alfredo.

The old man chuckled. "You have to admit I was a good-looking young man, eh?"

Dani's jaw dropped, and he stared at the old man. His grandfather's face had broken into a thousand wrinkles and his two puffs of white hair were sticking merrily upwards.

Dani was still dumbfounded when his mother and grandmother burst into the room. He turned to them in a fury. "You knew all along? All the time . . . you knew?" he said, his voice choked with emotion.

"What did we know?" asked his mother gently. "That your grandfather was the Great Alfredo?"

Dani felt a tear trickle down his cheek.

The old man seemed to have woken from his hundred-year sleep and was watching the boy with interest. "Don't blame them," he whispered. "It was me. I wanted to forget the past."

Dani looked at his grandfather in surprise. A question was on the tip of his tongue, but the old man was already telling him the answer.

"It hurt too much to think that the world-famous Alfredo had turned into *this*," he said, gesturing with his old, trembling hands.

Without thinking, Dani reached for the gnarled old fingers. "But you could have taught me so much, Grandad!"

The old man fell back on his pillow and winked at him. "Well . . . I suppose it's never too late to start."

From that day on, Dani's grandfather entertained him with vivid stories about the good old days. As the manager of Alfredo's circus, he had travelled all over the world. Faraway cities and world-famous artists came to life in the

little back bedroom, and Dani felt at home among them. He could almost see himself getting up onto the elephant's back, scratching the lion's mane and bravely dangling from the trapeze as he performed death-defying stunts.

The most fascinating stories were those about the jugglers, and Dani resolved to practise every day. First, he tossed apples into the air and caught them. Then he tried oranges. When he started juggling with the eggs his grandmother had set aside for their Sunday cake, she announced that enough was enough. After that, Dani always carried two or three of the old juggling clubs in his rucksack, and the children in the schoolyard watched in amazement as he tossed them high in the air.

During the next few weeks, something changed. No one looked

for the reason why, but now Dani always had a partner at school, and he was one of the first to be picked for the football team. He kept on practising, and was happy to do his juggling tricks for anyone who wanted to see them. And plenty did – Dani had stopped being invisible.

To this day, Dani's street is filled with the scent of roses. If you should go that way, just close your eyes. It is the thirteenth house (just beyond the tower blocks) and you'll be able to find your way there even with your eyes closed.

Just follow the scent of roses.

Efi

Be Lucky, Batbayan!

Once upon a time there was a boy with brown eyes and skin the colour of chocolate. His name was Batbayan, and at the beginning of my story, he must have been about eight years old.

One sad day, Batbayan said to his father, "When's Mum coming back?"

Batbayan's father pulled him into his arms and wiped the boy's eyes with the sleeve of his sweater. "Whenever you look at something beautiful, Mum will be looking back at you from it. She'll be laughing in the stars and smiling from the flowers. Do you remember the blackbird we listened to

together in the forest? She's there singing with him now."

Time went by, and Batbayan's father became friendly with a pretty woman called Franciska. She seemed kind at first and it was not long before they were married. Although his new wife had twin sons of her own and often over-indulged them, it soon became obvious she didn't like Batbayan. The little boy did everything he could to please her, but she remained as unfriendly as ever.

Would she like me better if my skin were as white as hers and her sons'? wondered Batbayan.

Before long, Batbayan's father also left them for a better place. Batbayan's heart almost broke in two, and he was also angry at his father for leaving him alone.

"Dad! Where have you gone? Come back!" he cried bitterly.

Just then, a little stripy mouse appeared from goodness knows where. It climbed up onto Batbayan's shoulder and began to nudge him with its nose and tickle his neck with its whiskers. The little boy held his hand out flat for the mouse to climb onto and he looked at it carefully. The two black stripes on the mouse's coat were just like the two black streaks in his father's grey hair.

Batbayan felt much less alone. "You know what? I'll call you Tikno!" he said as he hugged the little creature to his chest. That had been his father's nickname too. "Do you fancy staying here with me?"

The little mouse looked up from where it stood on the boy's palm and nodded.

"We'll have to be careful that no one sees you, though," said the boy. *That won't be too hard,* he thought. Nowadays he was sleeping in the old washhouse – Franciska had turned his old room into a guest room after his father died

In time, all the boys grew up to be good-looking young men. Andris and Botond began to go out with the local girls, but Batbayan wasn't interested in that sort of thing. He was far happier spending his evenings at home, reading

or listening to music.

His stepmother couldn't stop herself from commenting on this. "Look at your brothers! Now they're setting a fine example, always bringing home beautiful girls to introduce to us. You've never even had one girlfriend!" She pestered him at every turn.

Whenever she did this, Tikno would pop out of his hole, as if he sensed that his friend needed him.

Days passed and weeks went by, until one day, Andris came home with some news.

"Listen!" he shouted in excitement. "The Liebherrs' son, Ottó, is organising a New Year's Eve ball and he's inviting anyone who is seventeen and lives in the area!"

"Let's hope you find a good match there!" said Franciska to her sons, clapping for joy.

Batbayan was glad to hear about the ball too, because he loved music. He hoped he would be able to go.

"Andris, Botond! Get ready! We need to buy you some new clothes! You can't go in last year's faded old things!" pronounced their mother, who was already getting into the car, forgetting all about her stepson.

When they got home, the three of them strutted about in front of the mirror, showing off their new clothes.

Batbayan plucked up his courage and went to his stepmother. "Franciska, I'd like to go to the ball. Will you buy me something smart to wear too?"

He stood there, awkwardly shifting his weight from one foot to the other, wearing a jacket and a pair of trousers he had outgrown long ago. He had tried pulling at them to stretch them, but they just wouldn't get any longer.

"You don't think I'm going to spend a fortune on you, do you? You should be glad I keep you at all! There, these should be big enough for you!" she said, throwing him the old clothes her burly sons had just taken off. They were so large, two Batbayans would have fitted into them.

Seething with rage, the boy marched off to his room. He didn't cry very often – he was ashamed of his tears even when he was the only one to see them. Everyone was always telling him that real men didn't cry, and he wanted to be a real, strong man.

Tikno ran up onto his shoulder, and whispered to him in his father's voice, "Cry all you want! Tears are good for you. They make you strong."

At that, fat, glistening drops began to roll down Batbayan's cheeks.

The big day came at last. Andris and Botond had been preening themselves in front of the mirror since morning, along with Franciska, who had been invited to a New Year's Eve party by some neighbours of the Liebherrs'.

Batbayan had been clinging to the hope that his stepmother would relent and let him go to the ball after all. His brothers were all too aware of this.

"Bati, wouldn't you like a suit as smart as this one?" teased Andris.

"Come here, I've got something for you," said Botond, following his brother's lead. He lured Batbayan towards him, only to pick three pebbles up from the ground and fling them at him.

"By the time we get back, our rooms had better be gleaming, cry baby!" he shouted with cruel glee.

Batbayan knew that if he didn't clean his pampered stepbrothers' rooms, they would keep on poking fun at him. At least if he cleaned them, the two boys would leave him alone for a while.

Without knowing why, he scooped up the three pebbles and laid them on his desk before putting on his favourite song and hurling himself down on his bed. Tikno poked his nose out, then crawled up to sit in the hollow of Batbayan's collarbone and nodded along to the music.

Batbayan was soon in a better mood. He grabbed a duster

and was about to get started on the cleaning when he noticed that the three pebbles were glowing with a yellow light.

He gently tapped one. It was warm to the touch. Then, to his astonishment, clothes – a beautiful dinner jacket, a light blue shirt, a pair of elegant black shoes and a bowtie – shot out of it.

"Cool!" he cried.

He touched his finger carefully to the second pebble, and suddenly a gorgeous, bronze-coloured limousine appeared in front of the house.

"Wahey!" whooped Batbayan.

Burning with curiosity he touched the third pebble, and a smartly dressed man leaped out.

"*T'aves baxtalo, Batbayan!* Be lucky, Batbayan! What a fine figure of a man you've become!" said the man, who was dressed in a black felt hat, embroidered waistcoat and dark green trousers, and sported a moustache. From his words and his outfit, Batbayan guessed he was a Roma.

"Who are you?" asked the boy, amazed.

"Tupka, at your service! Your great-great-great-uncle."

"My great-great-great-uncle?" said Batbayan, staring. "How is that possible?"

"After my death, I agreed to serve here on Earth, and I was given the task of protecting our family's young ones. I saw you were in trouble, so here I am."

Batbayan's little mouse was jumping around, eager to greet Tupka.

"Hey, old pal! Give me five!" cried Tupka, holding out his hand to slap Tikno's tiny paw.

Batbayan was more and more convinced he must be dreaming.

"Look at you with your mouth open! Trying to catch flies, are you? Well, do you want to go to the ball, or not?" pressed Tupka.

"I'm desperate to go!" said Batbayan.

"Then pull yourself together and get changed!"

"I've got to clean my stepbrothers' bedrooms. If I don't, they'll give me an even harder time."

"Come on now, where's your Gypsy spirit, my lad?"

Batbayan looked at his uncle, wide-eyed. What was he talking about?

"Ah, we'll come back to that later," said his uncle.

He snapped his fingers once, and the duster flew around, wiping down everything in the room. He snapped them twice and the vacuum cleaner, bewitched, leapt out of the cupboard and started to gobble up dust devils.

"Cool! Where did you learn to do that?" cried Batbayan, looking admiringly at his great-great-great-uncle.

"And for my last trick . . ." said this extraordinary relation, snapping his fingers three times. The bottle of cleaning fluid started to spray the windows, a cloth following along behind to polish the panes.

Batbayan stood and watched the performance, grinning from ear to ear, until his uncle chided him, "Stand there gaping any longer and you'll miss all the fun! Go, go, go!"

Batbayan scrambled into the smart clothes.

Tupka looked him up and down, frowning. "Something's still missing . . . Got it!" he cried. "A beard!"

He snapped his fingers a few times and drew a spiral in the air. In a matter of moments, the boy's chin was covered in a short, stylish beard.

"There you go! Now no one will know you from Adam, I swear!" said Tupka, very pleased with himself.

He ushered Batbayan into the bronze limousine and off they set for the Liebherrs' house, up on the hill.

Before the boy got out of the car, Tupka said, "Make sure you're back here by the car before midnight, otherwise they'll all know who you are. The spell lasts only till then."

"Got it! I'll be there," said Batbayan.

The mansion was elegant and spacious, filled with potted palms and huge vases of flowers, and the windows were hung with white-and-gold brocades, silk and lace. Out in the grounds was a beautiful lake full of colourful fish. A well-known rock band filled the space with lively music.

Carried away by all this elegance and feeling like a new person in his smart clothes (they really were a perfect fit!), Batbayan strode confidently into the ballroom. He was handed a glass of champagne and sipped it happily.

The highlight of the evening was karaoke, which Batbayan put his name down for. He chose an old Serbian folk song he had learned from his mother, and the rock band played a modern arrangement.

When he started to sing, the room fell so quiet you could hear a fly buzzing. Batbayan's voice swelled to fill the hall.

Ottó, the son of the host, was very curious about the stranger. When the young man had finished singing and the audience broke into thunderous applause, Ottó moved towards him. But he lost sight of the singer in the crowd.

What Ottó didn't know was that Batbayan was in a hurry. It was nearly midnight!

In his haste to get away, Batbayan managed to lose his bowtie, which had become loose and slipped off as he fled. Ottó found it by the flower-trimmed front door. He asked around, trying to find out more about the mysterious boy – who had captured his heart almost at first sight – but no one knew who he was.

Tupka and his nephew just managed to reach home before the limousine, the elegant clothes, the beard and Tupka himself vanished into thin air. Exhausted from his thrilling night, Batbayan fell asleep long before his stepbrothers and stepmother returned.

When the two boys went into their rooms, they marvelled at the shiny windows and gleaming woodwork. How clean everything was!

But the next day, as usual, the twins started to wind their stepbrother up. "Imagine! There was karaoke, and someone got up to sing – a guy with real talent – but no one knew who he was!"

Batbayan tried to keep a straight face. For the first time in his life, their words rolled off him like water off a duck's back.

Days passed and weeks went by, and the Liebherrs' son organised another ball. Batbayan hoped that the magic pebbles would help him once again, and that he would have another chance to meet his great-great-great-uncle.

His stepbrothers poked fun at him this time too. "Another ball! Can't wait! All those girls! Really good-looking ones too! What a shame you can't go!" they sniggered.

"This house had better look decent when we get back! I want it clean as a whistle from top to bottom!" Franciska called over her shoulder as they left.

"Decent indeed! If my father were alive, he'd show you what decency was!" fumed Batbayan silently, then went back to his room to listen to music.

Tikno settled into the hollow of Batbayan's collarbone and nodded to the rhythm of the song. The little mouse was as much of a music fan as Batbayan.

Before long, the pebbles began to glow again, just as Batbayan had hoped they would. This time they shone with an orange light, and when he touched the first one it felt much hotter than last time. When he ran his fingers over the veined surface of the stone, out sprang a dinner jacket, a beautiful pink shirt, a pair of elegant shoes and a bowtie. When he touched the second stone, a silver limousine appeared in front of the garage. Batbayan carefully reached out and touched the third stone, and out leaped Tupka.

"Ooh, I've got a stiff neck!" he said, having a stretch before greeting his nephew. "It's been a while, mate! Give me five!"

Tupka's hand came down on Batbayan's and then on

Tikno's little paw too. "What's going on? Have those posers gone off and left you here to do the cleaning again?"

Batbayan nodded and pulled a face.

"Never fear, I'm here!" cried Tupka and snapped his fingers loudly. A duster lying on the table began to dance, wiping clean everything in its path. He snapped his fingers twice more and the vacuum cleaner launched itself into the air. He snapped his fingers three times and, in an instant, the windows were sparkling.

"All done!" announced Tupka, looking very pleased with himself. "But we haven't got all day! Off you go and get dressed. I'll be waiting in the limousine."

Batbayan got ready as fast as he could and fell into the seat next to Tupka.

Soon they were parked in front of the Liebherrs' house. Batbayan's uncle turned to him. "Remember, you have to be here in the car before midnight because the spell only lasts till then!"

"I know, I know," replied Batbayan.

"Wait – one moment! We nearly forgot something."

The young man put his hand to his chin. "The beard!"

Tupka clicked his fingers and drew a spiral in the air, at which Batbayan's chin vanished under a handsome beard identical to the one before. "There we go! Now you're ready! Have a great time!"

"Thank you!" Batbayan shouted as the car sped away.

At this ball too, everyone was having a great time. Then came the most exciting part of the evening: the karaoke.

All the guests and the host's son, Ottó, were curious to see whether the young man with the amazing voice would step forward to sing again. When the mysterious stranger took his place on the stage, the crowd was delighted. For those few minutes, swept along by his magical performance, the guests sang as one. Their voices seemed to merge into one another, until they made a single, unified sound.

At that point, Batbayan noticed a pair of blue eyes looking at him with a particular warmth and intensity, and everything else around him faded away. The blue eyes, and the dark-blond hair hanging over them, were Ottó's.

Ottó couldn't explain it, but he felt that he absolutely must speak to the singer. He tried to keep his eyes on the mystery boy as he left the stage, but there was such a crush of people that he managed, once again, to lose sight of him. This time he found only a single cufflink that Batbayan had dropped at the door on his way out.

Next time, we'll meet for sure! thought Ottó.

Tupka dropped his nephew off at home exactly at midnight. He quickly waved goodbye and vanished, along with Batbayan's beard and the other elegant things.

The little mouse was standing up on his hind legs, waiting for his friend.

"Wow, Tikno! It was so, *so* good! Imagine – the audience sang along with me! Can you believe it?"

The mouse nodded eagerly and squeaked by way of reply.

"And that boy . . . Those blue eyes . . ."

By the time his stepmother and brothers arrived home, Batbayan was sleeping peacefully.

The next morning, Franciska looked her stepson up and down suspiciously. Botond and Andris started to taunt their brother again. "Oh, Bati, you should've been there! You should've seen how the crowd went crazy for that mysterious singer . . ."

Batbayan tried once again to keep the straightest of straight faces so as not to give himself away, but inside he was whooping for joy, and thinking, *If you only knew . . .*

Time went by and the two stepbrothers brought news of yet another ball at the Liebherrs' house. As usual, they teased their brother as they broke the news.

"What are you doing Saturday night, Bati?" asked Andris.

"*We're* going to a ball," boasted Botond. "Poor little Batbayan. He has nothing to wear, so he can't come and party with us."

"You just wait and see!" muttered their stepbrother under his breath.

Saturday evening came around and everyone assumed that Batbayan would be staying at home. His stepmother, who was also going to a ball, gave him plenty of housework to do as usual.

"You'll have time to clean the whole house from the cellar to the attic, and make sure you do more than flick a duster at it this time!" she admonished, and, chuckling at her own wit, she slammed the door behind her.

For a few moments, Batbayan listened as the tapping of her stiletto heels grew faint, then he put on his favourite music and, with Tikno on his shoulder, lay back on his bed. For once he was neither angry nor disappointed. He knew by now that a wonderful evening awaited him. He relaxed and enjoyed the music until the pebbles on his desk started to glow red.

Carefully, he touched the first. The stone was so hot, it almost burned his finger. Suddenly out shot a stylish dinner jacket, a white shirt, a pair of elegant shoes and a bowtie. He touched the second stone and – *whoosh!* – there in front of the garage was a gold limousine. And out of the third stone leapt his uncle, twirly moustache, black felt hat, and all.

"Batbayan, my mate!" he cried.

"Tupka! I knew you'd come!"

"Out with it then! What are you supposed to be doing instead of going to the ball?"

"Cleaning. Cellar to attic," replied the boy.

"Let's see, now . . ." said Tupka, and with a few clicks of his fingers, his hard-working clean-up team had the whole house gleaming. "That's the way! All done!" he said, clapping

his hands together. "Oh, before I forget . . ."

A few clicks and a spiral in the air grew a beard on his nephew's face. "Get your glad rags on! I'll be outside."

Batbayan was dressed and in the car in minutes.

They were soon at the Liebherrs' house.

"You know the rule: the spell lasts till midnight. So – be lucky, Batbayan!"

Even before he got to the door, Batbayan could hear the music drawing him in. He entered and sipped at his champagne with relish.

Once again, all evening Ottó searched for the mysterious stranger with the golden voice, but our friend had disappeared into the crowd.

Batbayan was already up onstage when Ottó finally spotted him. This time the young stranger chose a song that spoke to the heart, and he sang it straight to Ottó, who was determined not to let the singer get away from him this time. To make sure of it, he jumped up onto the stage and began to sing with him.

When the song was finished, the audience called the boys back for an encore, and they sang together a second time.

Batbayan was so carried away, he forgot to look at his watch. When at last he did, there were only a few minutes till midnight. He headed for the exit as fast as he could. But Ottó was on the lookout and managed to stay on his tail, overtaking him just as he reached the door. He grabbed Batbayan's arm and wouldn't let go.

The clock struck twelve, and there stood Batbayan in front of his elegantly dressed host and singing partner. His face was beardless, and he was dressed from head to toe in his shabby old clothes. His cheeks burned with shame.

"I'm sorry," he murmured.

"There's nothing to be sorry for! I'm just glad I can finally get to know you. I'm Ottó!" said his host, holding out his hand.

"Well, then, I'm glad too. My name's Batbayan," said the mystery singer, smiling.

The two boys talked and talked until morning. They had so much to say to each other, just like two old friends who hadn't seen each other for a long, long time.

When Andris, Botond and Franciska got back to the gleaming house, Batbayan was nowhere to be seen. They soon heard, however, that Ottó Liebherr had found the love of his life. When they heard it was Batbayan who would be living with him in that grand mansion, they were green with envy.

And it didn't help that Batbayan and Ottó's wedding feast was the grandest for many miles around.

I like to think they are still together, living a life of love and happiness and plenty. Who knows!

Petra Finy

Thumbelina Gets a Life

Some stories don't start where they are supposed to. They start where another story ends. This story is one of those.

Everyone knows how the story of Thumbelina ends: the little heroine escapes from the fieldmouse and from marriage to the dull, spiteful mole. The swallow she had nursed so constantly all through the winter comes back for her and whisks her away from these horrors just in time. He carries her to a land where tiny people just like her bob and sway in the flower-cups. And where does Thumbelina's friend the swallow put her down? Where else but on the petals of the flower in which the ruler of that unusual country lives, the super-handsome prince of the fairies.

Much to the prince's amusement, Thumbelina was amazed to find that there were other people as small as her, and that they were so beautiful too. For, there's no denying it, the little girl found the prince very pleasing to look at.

The prince was also attracted to Thumbelina, but perhaps he found the wonder in her eyes when she looked at him even more pleasing. He was used to his subjects bowing their heads to him, so what else would he expect?

Thumbelina turned to the prince with sincere, heartfelt love, and was as ready to give of herself as she had been in all her previous encounters. And the prince of the fairies thought this love was for him and him alone. It appealed to his vanity and was a very pleasant feeling indeed.

He wasted no time, therefore, in asking for his surprise visitor's hand in marriage. Then he announced that there would be a great fairy wedding feast. Thumbelina didn't want a big fuss, but for the sake of her future husband she put up with it.

She didn't notice that before the wedding the servants ran about doing only the prince's bidding, and that they spent more time working on curling the tassels of his wedding robe than on designing her entire wedding dress.

Right from the beginning, everything revolved around the prince. Thumbelina was no more than a pretty porcelain figure by his side, an ornament to be shown off, pleasant to boast about but too much trouble to truly bother with.

But the wedding was so magnificent, the lights so pretty, the fairy-music so soul-stirring and the fairies' dancing so feather-light that she paid little attention to the way he was treating her. The wedding feast was sumptuous. The whole fairy empire came together to celebrate, and the bride was touched to see how delighted the guests all were. She didn't notice that her new husband hadn't once looked into her eyes, hadn't once smiled at her.

Then came the flat, grey everyday.

The fairy prince paid even less attention to Thumbelina than he had before. He spent all day in front of the mirror, admiring himself, never so much as glancing in her direction. He spent hours trying on one new cloth-of-gold suit after another and getting his hair styled in new ways. He was continually trying out new royal sports for his own entertainment and being applauded for his skill by his servants.

Somehow, though, he always forgot to invite his young wife to come and watch him.

Every morning, with the same tender-hearted kindness, Thumbelina would set down his fairy scrambled eggs before him and fill his glass with heavenly ambrosia. The prince, however, never concerned himself with her. As disappointment followed disappointment, the light in the young wife's eyes gradually faded, and the prince ceased

to be interested in her at all. He went in search of other eyes to look admiringly at him, other gazes in which to bask.

Thumbelina didn't understand why the prince wasn't nice to her, when she was so kind to him. After a while, he began not only to look right through her, but also to mock her and malign her.

"How come you're so small?" he would demand, even though he was no bigger than she was.

"What's with the sarcastic face?" he would say, when Thumbelina was only smiling at him nicely.

"Why do you have to be so sneaky?" he would ask, even though his wife would have been given a real dressing-down if she dared to disagree with him.

"Why is the apple pie so hot? Why is the apple pie so cold? Why are we having apple pie at all?

You're always dragging your feet; it hurts my ears! You creep around so quietly – spying on me, are you? Your hair looks like you've been dragged through a hedge backwards – is that what a fairy princess should look like? Your hair is plaited too tightly – why do you have to act all superior in front of my subjects? Why are you always putting in your two pennyworth, when you have no idea about royal affairs? Why do you sit there dumbly when your lord and master is asking for advice on matters of state?"

He found fault with every gesture Thumbelina made, with everything she said, with even the smallest thing she did. She had no idea any more of what she would have to do to get a word of praise from him. She was more and more confused by his contradictory instructions and his insults.

Thus it was that Thumbelina, who had always had a radiant smile and a light step, began to wilt. She lost her cheerful nature, the light faded from her previously bright spirit, and a shadow fell across her. A grey veil descended over her face, her body and her whole life.

One day, Thumbelina thought she saw a small piece of that veil fall to the ground. But it was not a piece of grey material. It was a glossy bird's feather.

The feather belonged to Thumbelina's own dear swallow, who always appeared when she was in trouble. She didn't even need to call him. He always knew if she was unhappy. He could see it in her eyes, which dragged him down like a dark, bottomless well.

The swallow flew down to his friend, who threw her arms around his neck as she had in the old days. She was silent, as by that time she had run out of words. She just rubbed her wet cheeks against his chest, and a few tears, as bright and clear as diamonds, found their way in between the bird's feathers. The grey veil had floated away as soon as she embraced her friend.

When the swallow asked her if she wanted to come away

with him, far away from this glittering but unhappy fairy life, Thumbelina's misery evaporated almost completely.

She clung onto the swallow's back and held tightly onto his neck.

She let the wind blow the sorrow out of her hair.

She let the sun shine light into her soul.

She let her face open up in a smile.

"After everything that's happened, how will I know whom I should love, little swallow, tell me that?" mused Thumbelina, when they were far away from the fairy empire.

"Well, perhaps you could choose someone who wants you, not someone who loves what they see of themselves in you," the swallow pointed out gently. "I can't always be there to rescue you. You have to learn to help yourself!"

Thumbelina nodded.

And indeed it wasn't long before Thumbelina did learn how to help herself. However small she might be, at last she felt big enough to live her life.

Krisztina Rita Molnár

The Bird with the Ruby-Red Feathers

The story I'm going to tell you is about much more than a red bird. There is a bird in it, but in order for this bird to be able to fly up into the sky and cleave the clouds on its ruby-red wings, and for us finally to hear its piercing song, there's a whole lot of other things I need to tell you about.

To start with, I should say that this is not a story that I made up. It's an old tale from faraway Greece, from the times when the kings themselves took their sheep out onto the hillsides to graze. I'm telling it to you because I think it is a beautiful story, one that is strange and sad, and gives you a lot to think about.

Caenis was a beautiful girl, so radiant, so dazzling, as we say in our Hungarian fairy tales, that it was easier to look at the sun than to look at her. She was born in Thessaly, on the shores of the Aegean Sea, so it was little wonder that she was beautiful. Her father, Elatus, raised her as a princess. Her mother, Hippea, taught her to sing, to twist her hair into ringlets and to collect honey. Lovely Caenis had many suitors. Young men travelled from other city-states, eager to marry her, so that as one suitor left, the next would already be at the gate, hoping Caenis would choose him. But the thing is, (and, yes, this does happen!) Caenis was not interested in securing a husband. She much preferred to be alone. To go for walks by herself along the seashore. She would eat a few honeyed walnuts for breakfast, pin a snow-white orange flower or a few wine-red oleander petals in her hair, then set off for the beach. When she was out alone, she could let her thoughts wander far from home too. She would dream of adventures, of sailing through storms at sea, of bracing herself against the wind like the bravest men on the ship. She dreamt of going on hunting expeditions and chasing after the deer and the other wild animals.

Down on the shore, Caenis would collect beautifully shaped pebbles and shells and sing the sweet songs her mother had taught her:

Ruby-red morning, how sweetly you greet me.
With honeyed songs I reply.
My heart and my voice are leaping for joy.
I feel like I could fly!

As she walked along the strand, Caenis wasn't bothered when the sand crept into her golden sandals and tickled the soles of her feet. From time to time, she would sit down on a large, flat stone, undo the strap of her sandals and shake out the shiny, rolling grains. Then she would go closer to the sea and dip first her hands and then her feet in the shallow, sun-warmed water. She loved the water. She loved how, under the surface, the colours of the pebbles were much brighter, and she liked watching the hermit crabs scuttling along the seabed and hiding among the pebbles. The water made the crabs' little legs look bigger, and magnified the spiral patterns on the snail shells and the ridges on the empty seashells that had been washed up along the shoreline.

Caenis was also afraid of the water. It was a giant that seemed to go on for ever. You could never be sure when its waves would turn angry, when a storm would break. Then the seawater, stirred into madness, would leap up and the tongues of the waves would lick furiously at the mighty walls of rock that encircled the bay. Her mother, Hippea,

had often warned her to be careful when she went off walking alone, saying that the sea, just like its lord – trident-bearing Poseidon – was unpredictable. Anything unpredictable was dangerous, Hippea told her, and it was better to keep your distance. But Caenis didn't take her mother's advice very seriously. Her curiosity was stronger than her fear. *I know how to take care of myself,* she thought, shrugging her shoulders rebelliously. *There's so much to discover in the sea and, who knows, maybe one day I might even get to meet Poseidon himself!*

One day Caenis set off boldly for the sea as usual, hoping to find new treasures. She had pinned a red hibiscus flower in her ebony hair, her face was coral pink from the wind and her lips glistened from her breakfast of honey. She couldn't have predicted that trident-wielding Poseidon would, that very morning, choose to relax in her own dear bay. It was still high tide, so the water was deep over the soft sand. Caenis stopped at the water's edge, intending to wait for the tide to go down. She always enjoyed watching the tide retreat, was fascinated by how the water left the sand as smooth as if someone had spread a scarf of woven linen over it. The tide also left the strand littered with colourful seashells, sea-urchin skeletons and cuttlebones, all the treasures the sea carried up to her from its depths. For her alone. So she could collect them in her basket, then take them to her sisters and trade them for oranges and pomegranates. Her sisters liked to string the shells into necklaces or belts.

When Poseidon, the lord of the sea, saw this beautiful girl approaching, singing as she came, he was flooded by desire. It poured into every salty drop of his being, and he felt a desperate urge to put his arms around her.

So, rather than drawing back slowly and steadily as was usual after high tide, the sea did something it had never done before. It followed the orders of its lord Poseidon and stayed on the shore, lapping at Caenis's toes.

Then, the enormous, blue-haired god of the sea rose up out of the water.

"Welcome to the borders of my kingdom. I see that you like to venture close to the water. Such boldness! But I do not wonder at it. The sea is not without its dangers, but it is a dominion full of marvels. And you, my dear, are also to be marvelled at! Your ringlets are glossier than any black sea-snail. And your lips! No glowing pink coral can compare! Let me kiss them, just once, and I will give you anything you ask for. You have my word."

Caenis was terrified – but only for a moment. She remembered her mother's words, but in her mind's eye, she had already shrugged them off. She even smiled to herself, just a little, careful not to let Poseidon see.

"Greetings, O mighty sea god, great Poseidon! May I really choose anything at all? she asked, playing for time.

"It is rare to find a mortal as beautiful as you. So I have decided to grant you a wish, anything you ask for. What is your heart's desire? Just say the word – it's yours. I can deny you nothing!"

"You swear?"

"My word is my bond."

"All right. I believe you, Lord of the Raging Waters," replied Caenis. "If you grant my wish, I will grant yours."

"Out with it then!" the impatient god urged her.

Words came tumbling out of Caenis's mouth, like pine nuts rolling out of a pinecone on a hot summer's day.

"At first I thought I would ask you to give me your trident, the one you use to raise storms and calm them. How powerful I would be, if I could just hold it in my hand! But I don't want to be greedy. All I ask is that you turn me into a man!"

For a moment or two, Poseidon was stunned. He had not reckoned on such a request. Even the winds dropped to nothing. But a god has to keep to his word. The God of the

Sea nodded slowly. His blue locks fell onto his forehead.

"I understand what you are asking for," he answered.

By the time he raised his eyes again, they no longer fell on Caenis, but on an athletic young man.

Poseidon looked the young man over carefully. "I release you from your side of the bargain," he added, sadly.

"Thank you," came the answer in a deep, male voice. Because it was no longer Caenis standing there, but Caeneus, in men's clothes. His delicate girl's body had disappeared. The muscles in his arms bulged like ripe pomegranates. He had become taller and his legs felt many times stronger. But his black curls were as glossy and his lips still glowed the same coral-pink as when the god had first laid eyes on them.

"You'll be glad I wished for this, you'll see! And proud that you helped me," cried Caeneus.

Not for nothing was Poseidon immortal – he knew the boy was right. So he gave him one more extra gift. He made Caeneus invulnerable, as if his body were clothed in iron, not skin, so that no mortal would be able to wound him.

Caeneus lived for years in this new body, untroubled, becoming such a hero that his name was added to those of the greatest heroes, the Argonauts. He embarked with these bravest of Greek warriors on the *Argo*, making a perilous voyage to take the golden fleece from the dragon that was guarding it. Caeneus was there when the Argonauts hunted down the terrible wild boar that Artemis had sent to ravage the region of Calydon, helping to bring down this monstrous creature.

I could go on listing Caeneus's glorious deeds, but for now, I will tell you about just one. This tale I must recount so that we can, at last, catch a glimpse of the bird with the ruby-red feathers that I promised you at the beginning. Perhaps you have already guessed that we are talking about Caeneus's final battle. The one that took place at the wedding feast of Pirithous, King of the Lapiths.

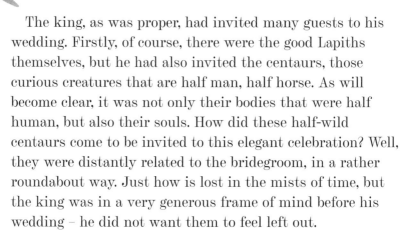

The king, as was proper, had invited many guests to his wedding. Firstly, of course, there were the good Lapiths themselves, but he had also invited the centaurs, those curious creatures that are half man, half horse. As will become clear, it was not only their bodies that were half human, but also their souls. How did these half-wild centaurs come to be invited to this elegant celebration? Well, they were distantly related to the bridegroom, in a rather roundabout way. Just how is lost in the mists of time, but the king was in a very generous frame of mind before his wedding – he did not want them to feel left out.

For a while, the celebration went on as it should. Honeyed wine flowed into the glasses of the guests. Oak tables were piled high with aromatic meat stews, olives and cheese platters, garnished with bunches of sweet grapes, pomegranates and oranges. Both the Lapiths and the centaurs were enjoying themselves, until . . . alas! How a single moment can spoil everything!

One of the centaurs had been drinking too much, and the raisin wine had gone to his head. (As his body was half horse, you could say the wine had made an ass out of him – though this does seem a little hard on donkeys!) Anyway, this centaur had lost all sense of what was proper. Having taken a fancy to the king's young bride, Hippodamia, he moved towards her like a poacher intent on his prey. Weaving along as unsteadily as a sheep with the staggers, he crashed into her. He stared at the young woman with blurry eyes, then suddenly reached towards her, grabbed her saffron-coloured veil and ripped it away, neighing and laughing wildly in her face.

That was enough for the heroic Lapiths, among them our Caeneus. They leapt up from the table and rushed to the young bride's defence. Yes, but the centaurs also rose to their feet, and, overturning the plates, leaped over to join their brother. What happened next is not easy to describe.

Imagine a wedding feast transformed into a battleground! Hippodamia and her bridesmaids fled into the farthest nook of the greenery-decked cave. The warriors and the centaurs struck and sliced at each other, forgetting their duty as guests, casting a shadow over the bright feast. By the end they had forgotten how it all started and were fighting for their very lives, slashing at each other so fiercely they began to drop like flies. Many were the centaurs, and young Lapith men, who fell in that terrible battle. Caeneus fought too, his strength swollen by a sudden, painful rage. One of the centaurs, Latreus by name, seeing that Caeneus had already beaten off five centaurs, began to taunt him, making fun of his past.

"Hey, Caenis, I heard you were born a girl. What are you doing here with us heroes? I can't stand the sight of you. A little snivelling thing you were, and you're still a girl as far as I'm concerned. Fighting's not for the likes of you! Go and spin some thread. You'd be better with a basket in your hands than a weapon!"

At these words, Caeneus's rage burned white-hot. He flew at Latreus with a spear. The centaurs, however, knowing that Caeneus' body was invulnerable, had other ideas.

"Stick him in the ground! Bury him up to his waist! Pile stones and great trees on top of him – that's the way! Cover him up so we never have to look at him again. Get rid of him before he beats us all!"

They did more than threaten. They got straight to work, pulling oak trees and pines out of the stony ground, roots and all, and throwing boulders on top to make a rocky outcrop. Intending to crush Caeneus's last breath out of him, they worked tirelessly, piling rocks and trees on top of him until they were satisfied that their plan had succeeded.

What they didn't know, however, was that clear-sighted Mopsus, a Lapith hero standing sorrowfully by the heap of stones and trees that covered his friend, had noticed something that he would only tell his companions one quiet evening much later.

In that terrible moment after the battle, it was as if a thick mist had descended on the survivors in their spoiled wedding finery. Nothing could be seen of Caeneus, buried under the forest of trees. But all of a sudden, from the midst of the oak branches covering his head, a beautiful bird with ruby feathers had flown up into the sky. A bird with ruby-red feathers! Singing!

Ruby-red morning, how sweetly you greet me.
With honeyed songs I reply.
My heart and my voice are leaping for joy.
I feel like I could fly!

Never before or since had Mopsus seen a bird like it. At that moment, he knew exactly who it was soaring freely over the heads of the Lapiths and the centaurs, his powerful song reaching far into the sky.

Zoltán Csehy

A Princely Wedding

Based on the picture book King & King, *by Linda de Haan and Stern Nijland, rewritten and turned into a poem by Zoltán Csehy.*

Three golden hills away from here,
And over the silver mountain,
Where the short-tailed piglet wallows and wades
In the splashing silver fountain,
There lived a prince, his mother, Pat,
Along with the palace tabby cat,
As cosy as can be, all three.
(Listen well as my tale I tell.)
As cosy can be.

The prince's mum was getting old,
And weary of her throne.
From morning to night she'd bend his ear,
"It's time to retire," she'd groan.
"I'd like to stroll the palace grounds,
And patch up all my favourite gowns.
Now, that's the life for me, you see!"
(Listen well as my tale I tell.)
"That's the life for me!"

The weeks went by, until the queen,
Frustrated, lost her head.
She went to her handsome, princely son,
And dragged him out of bed.

"Useless, feckless lad of mine,
It's time you found a bride.
You must rule this land!" she cried.
(Listen well as my tale I tell.)
"You must rule!" she cried.

Blinking, the prince could see she meant it,
No more could he say, "We'll see."
Stunned, he fumbled and dropped his phone,
Couldn't stomach his toast and tea.
The determined queen set out her plan
To make her son a married man.
His royal rank, she said, required it.
(Listen well as my tale I tell.)
His royal rank required it.

"Every prince for miles around
Has married – long ago.
They're busy ruling, riding to battle . . .
Where is *your* princely show?
Even the feeble or shy are married.
None of those bad-looking ones have tarried.
You're the only one who bides his time."
(Listen well as my tale I tell.)
"The one who bides his time."

The queen, she shrieked and wept and wailed,
Till he vowed he would contrive it.
If he *really* had to, he would wed.
Others, he knew, had survived it!
His happy mother gave him a kiss
And called every maiden on her list.
(Listen well as my tale I tell.)
Every maiden on her list.

The princesses came, an endless stream,
A vast and amazing crowd.
Sofia, the diva, from Salzburg sang,
Her soaring voice . . . *so* loud.
When she warbled with ease those very high Cs,
The luckless prince, his blood did freeze.
(Listen well as my tale I tell.)
The prince, his blood did freeze.

Dressed in white, like a sizeable swan,
She added glissandos and trills.
But though her cadenzas were second to none,
The prince was unmoved by her skills.
If she sang again, he solemnly swore,
He'd shun the opera for ever more.
(Listen well as my tale I tell.)
He'd shun it for ever more.

Dolly was next – from Texas she came,
And juggled as well a clown.
She kept six balls in the air at once,
Not a single one fell down!
But though she dazzled from dusk till dawn,
All the prince could do was yawn.
(Listen well as my tale I tell.)
All he could do was yawn.

A princess from Greenland turned up next –
Even her *skin* was green.
She hoped it would impress the prince,
Enough to make her his queen.
But the daughter of that vegan king,
From this young prince would acquire no ring.
(Listen well as my tale I tell.)
She would acquire no ring.

From distant Mumbai came an elegant model,
Decked from head to toe,
In Gucci and Prada, Versace and more,
Fresh from a catwalk show.
But in the prince, she inspired no passion,
Despite his keen interest in fashion.
(Listen well as my tale I tell.)
Despite his interest in fashion.

Straight from the Great Hungarian Plain
Came a horsewoman, hat, whip and all.
She could round up foals, her goulash was great,
And she even had a cowboy drawl.
But her pancakes left the prince unmoved.
They never really got into the groove.
(Listen well as my tale I tell.)
They never got into the groove.

Physicists came, astronomers too
With awards, diplomas, degrees.
Poets and scientists boasting MAs,
Philosophers with PhDs.
But although they had education in spades
In the prince's exam, none quite made the grade,
(Listen well as my tale I tell.)
None of them quite made the grade.

For the poor young prince there was no escape
As hard as he might try.
He felt like a butterfly run right through
By the pin of his mum's steely eye.
But the master of ceremonies wasn't yet done,
There was one last princess still to come.
(Listen well as my tale I tell.)
One last princess to come.

Into the room stepped a blonde princess.
With a smile, she let down her hair.
Fair-haired too was the brother beside her
In an instant, the young prince was snared!
What bliss was this? Joy beyond measure!
Here was a love he could finally treasure.
(Listen well as my tale I tell.)
A love he could finally treasure.

"The flame in my heart opens up like a rose.
I've not felt this fever before.
Here is my darling, here is my love,
The one I've been waiting for!"
The prince, all flustered and red in the face,
Reached out his arms for a loving embrace.
(Listen well as my tale I tell.)
Reached out for a loving embrace.

"I never did dare to imagine or think
That my mum's matrimonial schemes
Would make my life rich where once it was poor,
And send me *the man of my dreams*."
So now, in front of the royal household
The two princes' arms did each other enfold.
(Listen well as my tale I tell.)
Their arms did each other enfold.

The small princess looked on with a smile,
Glad for the joy of her brother.
He, not she, was the choice of the prince –
But *her* eye had been drawn by another . . .
The master of ceremonies had won her heart,
For our best-laid plans can still fall apart.
(Listen well as my tale I tell.)
Our plans can still fall apart.

What a grand and glorious wedding they had.
The young princes made a fine pair.
On the way to the altar, neither man faltered,
And eternal love met them there.
Even the church mouse, prone to a sneer,
Was said by observers to shed a small tear.
(Listen well as my tale I tell.)
Was said to have shed a small tear.

Afterword

by Dorottya Rédai, Project Coordinator
Labrisz Lesbian Association

This is a book of familiar stories with a difference.
It is the first Hungarian-authored children's book which
contains LGBTQ+ characters. However, this beautiful book
is not *only* a collection of LGBTQ+ fairy tales. It brings
a variety of identities and experiences closer to children.
It is not a 'catalogue' of minorities; some experiences may
be missing. These stories come from, and reflect, a Central
Eastern European socio-cultural milieu. They are pieces of
literature, as diverse as their authors.

Still, I believe that these tales will enchant children
in every corner of the world. They address issues that
any child could face, including discrimination and
acceptance, exclusion and inclusion, disadvantage and
privilege, unfairness and justice, race, class, gender
and sexuality, adoption, neglect, bullying and poverty.
They are also about love, happiness, magic, exploring
and finding one's true self, solidarity, supporting those
in need, respect, empowerment and freedom.

As a children's book containing LGBTQ+ characters, this
collection scandalized Hungarian politics on publication
in 2020 and gained enormous popularity both in
Hungary and abroad. Among the ten foreign languages
the book has been published in to date, the English
edition has its specific importance, as it will deliver the
stories to children and adults worldwide and earn its
deserved place in world's children's literature.

Dorottya Rédai